OUT HERE

OUT HERE

A NEWCOMER'S NOTES *from the*

GREAT NORTHWEST

ANDREW WARD

VIKING

VIKING
Published by the Penguin Group
Viking Penguin, a division of Penguin Books USA Inc.,
375 Hudson Street, New York, New York 10014, U.S.A.
Penguin Books Ltd, 27 Wrights Lane, London W8 5TZ, England
Penguin Books Australia Ltd, Ringwood, Victoria, Australia
Penguin Books Canada Ltd, 2801 John Street,
Markham, Ontario, Canada L3R 1B4
Penguin Books (N.Z.) Ltd, 182–190 Wairau Road,
Auckland 10, New Zealand

Penguin Books Ltd, Registered Offices:
Harmondsworth, Middlesex, England

First published in 1991 by Viking Penguin,
a division of Penguin Books USA Inc.

1 3 5 7 9 10 8 6 4 2

Earlier versions of these commentaries aired on National Public Radio's *All Things Considered* on the following dates: "That Bainbridge Island Attitude" on September 15, 1988; "The Visitor" on September 21, 1988; "Prey" on September 26, 1988; "Dogs in the Road" on October 6, 1988; "Miranda Mouse" on October 17, 1988; "Crops" on October 26, 1988; "Honk" on November 11, 1988; "Spa Defender" on November 23, 1988; "The Whale Watch" on January 5, 1989; "Oil and Water" on January 11, 1989; "Rainier" on March 27, 1989; "Silver and Gold" on May 29, 1989; "Ralph" on June 6, 1989; "Drew" on June 21, 1989; "Far West" on July 18, 1989; "Bum Fish" on August 14, 1989; "Boat Sick" on August 17, 1989; and "Parents Night" on September 7, 1989.

Some of the essays first appeared in different form in the following periodicals: "The Gazzam House" in *American Heritage;* "A Few Words of Wisdom to Husbands and Wives" as "Words of Wisdom for Husbands and Wives"; "The Essaymatic 5000"; "Yumbo"; "A Classic Confrontation" and "They Also Wait Who Stand and Serve Themselves" in *The Atlantic;* "The Bedtime Story" and "Fantasia" in *Parent's Choice;* and "The Movable Feast" as "The Christmas Feast" in *Food & Wine.*

LIBRARY OF CONGRESS CATALOGING IN PUBLICATION DATA
Ward, Andrew, 1946–
Out here : a newcomer's notes from the great Northwest / Andrew Ward.
p.   cm.
ISBN 0–670–83158–1
1. Bainbridge Island (Wash.)—Social life and customs.   2. Puget Sound Region (Wash.)—Social life and customs.   3. Ward, Andrew, 1946–   .   4. Bainbridge Island (Wash.)—Biography.   I. Title.
F897.K5W29 1991
979.7—dc20   90–50429

Printed in the United States of America
Set in Garamond #3
Designed by Fritz Metsch

FOR

DEBBIE, JAKE, AND CASEY

With all my love

Preface

Walking near my home in Cornwall, Connecticut, almost sixteen years ago, I came upon a goshawk's nest. The goshawk looks as bold as a bald eagle, with its white breast and eye stripe and Confederate-gray wings. But it is even more furtive and shy, and chooses its residence with aristocratic exclusivity.

I think I must have heard the goshawk shriek before I even saw her, and I didn't see her until it was almost too late: just as she was about to rake my head with her outstretched talons for blundering too close to her nest. Darting off the trail like a refugee fleeing a strafing, I ducked into some brush and watched the hawk swoop back to her nest fifty feet up in the branches of a white pine and land with a dismissive flick of her speckled wings.

From my remove I could just make out the feeble gray heads of two fledglings begging their mother for a chunk of my scalp. It took her half an hour to weary of their insistent cries, and after she'd flown off to fix them dinner, I crept up to the foot of her nesting tree and found the tiny bones of unlucky mice and squirrels scattered among the needles and wintergreen along the forest floor.

According to my copy of *Birds of North America,* the goshawk is uncommon to rare, and so I called up a friend of mine who was a birder, and we went out to photograph the hawk. Then he must have made some calls of his own, because within a few days flocks of local birders had begun to congregate in my neighbors' woods with their life lists and their binoculars, and within a week the wary goshawk had fled her public and abandoned her young and vacated the forest forever.

I will not claim that we wreak more devastation with our love than with our indifference, but sometimes I worry that the Northwest is like that goshawk, and that by writing about it and talking about it on Public Radio I endangered the very splendors I praised.

I conceive of myself not as a propagandist but rather as a writer, and as such I am in the thrall not of an agenda but a compulsion. I wrote most of these commentaries simply to record my sense of dislocation and discovery as a newcomer to the Northwest.

But as soon as I began to broadcast on *All Things Considered,* I heard from local listeners who were afraid I was imperiling Bainbridge Island, the state of Washington, the entire Northwest with my sometimes ecstatic descriptions of my newfound home. I tried to assure them, and myself, that no listener would be so impressionable as to move on my say-so to the remotest corner of the contiguous United States. It seemed to me that if some husband and father were to hop out of his car one evening in Chicago and declare to his family that they were Northwest-bound because of something he'd heard on Public Radio, he would be quietly sedated, and perhaps even institutionalized, long before he could call the movers.

"And I like to think," I heard myself tell one woman, "that if somebody did move out here, at least it might be for the right reasons."

But I've always been suspicious of whatever I like to think, and I still wonder if there was something I didn't understand about the power of the broadcast word. Some nights when the devil gets in, I wonder if for all my best intentions I *should* have shut up about it, or moved away, or gone into some other line of work.

Writers are vulnerable to this kind of stuff because, being egomaniacs, we're as likely to overestimate the damage we do as the good we do. Long before I got here, the local Department of Self-Fulfilling Prophecies had already announced that the population of Puget Sound was expected to double by the year 2000. Of course, all through the present century the year 2000 has lent itself rather conveniently to factors of two, and every day, it seems, somebody is predicting the doubling of something or other by the next millennium.

In any case, I wonder what exactly the rest of us are supposed to do with these predictions. Prepare for their fulfillment, I guess, just as we're supposed to prepare for the next earthquake. But earthquakes are natural and inexorable, and the kind of growth they're projecting is commercial and manmade and thus, presumably, a tad more exorable than plate tectonics. Preparing for an earthquake doesn't influence whether or not there is going to be an earthquake, but some preparations for growth seem to have a way of ensuring growth. In fact, a lot of what passes out here for preparations for growth—commissioning blueprints for malls, marinas, highways, transit systems, bridges, and golf course communities—actively promotes it.

When I arrived on Bainbridge Island, there were about three hundred and fifty houses available on the local market. A year later the inventory was down to one hundred and fifty, and another six months later there were only seventy houses available. Throughout western Washington the newspapers are filled with controversies over mass developments on lumber company land, and some of my neighbors—and no one can blame them at these prices—are cashing in on the influx of Californians looking for a residential upgrade in which to shelter themselves, their families, and their capital gains.

So it seems to a good many northwesterners that a lot of people, including myself, have prepared for growth elsewhere in the country by moving out here. To longtimers our attraction to the Northwest is an inevitable and ominous sociological phenomenon. We have come here to flee the mess we made back home. Stuck in traffic on the Connecticut Thruway, recovering from a mugging at Yale/New Haven Hospital, choking on pollution on the New Jersey shore, I must have come upon some reckless mention of Bainbridge Island on a list of Best Places to Live, or I must have caught sight of it somehow on television or in some back issue of *National Geographic,* and in the sway of a glimpse or a mention I moved my family and all my possessions three thousand miles from home.

But people are generally neither that impulsive nor that deliberate. Nor are most people I know back East all that miserable or restless. In fact, it would surprise a lot of northwesterners to know that few people, even when you include those who are aware of the Northwest's existence in the first place, have the slightest intention of moving here.

Take me, for example. When my wife began casting around for a job, I tried with all my wit and energy to convince her to find one in the Northeast, which was our home and remains home to most of my friends and family. I moved to the Northwest because my wife got a job at the University of Washington. And I was introduced to Bainbridge Island by a novelist friend who happened to live here and invited me out to the island one evening for supper. But for the job, we wouldn't have moved to the Northwest, and but for that friend we wouldn't have moved to Bainbridge Island.

I imagine that's what happens with most people. We new-comers may claim that we moved here to get away from something, but that's usually hindsight talking, not design. It's characteristically American to believe otherwise, but most people these days don't choose where they move and don't move where they choose. What's really fueling growth in western Washington is the economy: a robust Boeing Com-pany, the promise of trade with the phantasmagoric Pacific Rim, a growing contingent of high technologists, and what-ever trickles down therefrom.

So for the first time in a long while the Northwest is pros-perous. But prosperity seems a dicey proposition in a region that once offered so many riches money could not buy. The desert may excite a man's thirst for irrigation, the Great Plains may suggest unending fields of wheat, but western Washing-ton draws out the protective urge in all of us because the mountains and waters of Puget Sound can't be improved upon by commerce—only wounded and polluted.

Because we newcomers seem to be a consequence of pros-perity we are hard put to justify ourselves. Anybody who chooses to work me over on this score can make me feel awful about joining the squeeze on the Great Northwest. It's a guilt that feeds on my dislocation, I suppose, for it comes over me most powerfully when I'm pining for my home back East.

But at least I didn't clear a lot and build a new house out here, nor did I initially add to the total population, either. In fact, I effected a demographically even trade, because, like Debbie and me, the previous owners of our house had two children, and they vacated not only the house and the island but the entire Northwest for the milk and honey of old New York. And on the very day of our arrival my novelist friend moved not just out of the Northwest but out of the country, so that it can be said in my defense that I haven't even padded the region's literary profile.

Except for buying a few airline tickets and a couple of Washington State fir studs, I didn't have much to do with this century's ravages in the region. In fact, they were for the most part the work of the ancestors of the proprietary long-timers whose roots now flourish in the soil their grandfathers lumbered and slash-burned and regraded, and some of whom still occasionally call me up, usually at the dinner hour, to tell me where to go.

If a newcomer's love is always unrequited, so be it; I have languished in the grip of more than one infatuation. And nothing seems worthier of my pining and my heartbreak than the shy splendors of this beleaguered region.

But if what follows acquires a perch in your imagination, let it nest there undisturbed, lest we scare away the wary hawks of the Great Northwest. Decline whatever invitation I may seem to whisper in these pages, and accept these bits and pieces for what I intend them to be: the pleas and ruminations of a middle-aged man adrift in a world of perils and wonders.

Contents

Contents

OUT HERE

Realty

BEING a writer, I'm supposed to be portable, but I am like one of those thirty-five-pound typewriters that come with a strap. Though I can write pretty much anywhere they put me, by nature I am a nester from a long line of nesters: housebound, house-proud, house-poor.

I was born in Chicago and raised in India, but I've spent the rest of my life in Connecticut, where both of my children were born, and I fancy myself as much of a Connecticut Yankee as the original Andrew Ward of the family, my great-great-etc.-grandfather, who pioneered the Connecticut coast in the 1600s.

For me the authentic, the resonant, the familiar extends only so far as Connecticut's old Western Reserve in Ohio, beyond which the country seems to dissolve in the glare of the western sun. So when it began to look as though my wife was determined to accept a job on the West Coast, I tried desperately to get somebody to tell me that moving west would ruin my career.

But nobody would come through for me.

"There are lots of good writers out there," my brother told me.

"I think it might do you a world of good," my editor said.

OUT HERE

"You know, Andy," my agent gently suggested, "it's not as though they're gonna miss you at Elaine's."

Nonetheless, I was convinced that if I moved beyond commuting distance of New York City, not to mention Boston or Chicago, or even Denver, for Christ's sake, I would actually dematerialize, until all that was left of me was an outdated entry in a remaindered volume of *Books in Print.* So I encouraged Debbie to poke around for a job in Boston, and even when she was offered a lousy little research job in the wake of some self-described Great Man in Connecticut, I told her not to reject it out of hand.

But soon she was getting offers from all over the country, and, seeing what I was up to, she drew the line in the sand between us. If I would not move to Bloomington, Indiana, or Tempe, Arizona, or even Ann Arbor, Michigan (and I wouldn't), the choice boiled down to Los Angeles or Seattle.

After two decades of gift subscriptions to *Sunset* from my Californian in-laws, and despite some deranged fantasies of my own about directing movies, I thought I knew enough about L.A. to know I could not live there. (I guess my conception of the place boiled down to an article I once read by a former Angelino who, driving his children to school early one morning, passed by a crucified corpse hanging in a neighbor's yard. I think he said that the yard's automatic sprinklers were on as he drove past, but I may have added that detail myself.)

So one day in April of 1987 I flew off to the state of Washington, as determined as a groom in an arranged marriage to fall in love with the inevitable.

For two days I toured Seattle in the eager keeping of a Realtor: a pretty, lip-glossed woman who drove me around in a spotless Taurus. She delivered her pitch in a Shirley Temple singsong—something along these lines:

Mr. Ward, we're coming now to an area that's really a neighborhood on the upswing, we think, with lots of younger double-incomes like yourselves moving in and giving these great old houses the good old T.L.C., and I just think we just might find just the kind of cozy old place you're looking for.

One of the advantages of this area is the wonderful public schools, but there are private schools available for those families seeking an accelerated educational alternative. I know one of the gals in our office sends her boy to the Bush School, and she couldn't be happier with how it's working out.

This whole shopping area we're passing is new, of course, and several very fine restaurant franchises have opened here for the busy family, plus all the boutiques your wife will ever need.

Now, if you just look out your window you'll see the house coming up on your right. Isn't it nice? It's been on the market for a while, but it's really quite charming now that the police are all done with it. There's a lien on the pool, as I understand it, something about community access I think it was, but it's gonna be a real icebreaker with the neighbors.

She seemed a lot like the real estate agents I knew in New Haven; indeed, there was a lot about Seattle that reminded me of my neighborhood back home: the cracked sidewalks, the streets dense with trees and vines. Maybe I was just trying to make the best of things, but it seemed as though the authentic, the resonant, the familiar had somehow leapfrogged eighteen hundred miles of alien territory and taken root in the northwestern corner of the lower forty-eight.

In fact, I lost track of how far from home I was until we pulled out onto the rain-slick highway and a man in a truck tried to pass us in the middle of one of my Realtor's monologues.

"No *way*," she suddenly snarled, stepping hard on the accelerator, and we lurched forward, leaving the trucker in our spray.

"Oh dear," she said when I gaped at her, "I guess you're seeing my aggressive side."

She was thus the first of a particular variety of western woman I have since come to know well—what we used to call "hard candy" back in high school: cute, sweet, immaculate, and tough enough to break your teeth. (I now pass them every day along the island roads, walking briskly in pastel jogging ensembles, with perky bangs and little silver barbells.)

We spent a couple of days together pursuing a vision of mine that had been born of *Five Easy Pieces*—an old cottage with a lot of windows overlooking the water. Any water at all would do, as far as I was concerned: Lake Union, Lake Washington, Puget Sound, even the Pacific Ocean, which I somehow believed was close by.

But at first the Realtor kept taking me to spanking new houses in gated developments instead—carpeted monstrosities within earshot of freeways and shopping centers—or to mildewed lakeside cottages with stained walls of peeling veneer and warped shelves lined with cocktail tumblers.

So I gave up on my waterfronting cottage dream and decided to settle on a rough equivalent of our home back in New Haven, an ivied turn-of-the-century house on a residential city street, despite another Realtor's reassurances about the neighborhood.

"You're a writer?" she asked. "And your wife's a nurse? Oh, then you'll *adore* your neighbors," she said. "They're all doctors and anchorpersons."

But just before I was to fly home, I went out to visit an old friend on Bainbridge Island, a half hour's ferry ride from Seattle, where, pushing apart some roadside foliage in the evening light, he showed me the house I'd been looking for: authentic and resonant and strangely familiar even at first sight, a homely house of stone looking westward across the sound.

It seemed a wonderful house, and a wonderful house it has turned out to be, but maybe what I like best about it is that a Realtor didn't find it for me.

Yankee Provincial

W*HEN* I told Debbie we were going to live on an island, she gave me a look I hadn't seen cross her face since 1971, when I announced that everything in my life up to that moment—painting, photography, folk singing, writing—had been leading to one thing: movie directing.

For a moment her eyes darted around as if looking for an exit, as if I had suddenly caught fire, perhaps, or a venereal disease. She had waited out my movie-directing ambitions, but this time she recognized that I could fall in love with the Northwest only if I could fall in love with a house in the Northwest. So, after a week of phone calls to bankers, lawyers, prospective neighbors, school principals, and building engineers, we laid our money down.

Like an unfaithful husband returned from a fling, I felt that some basic attachment to the East had already come loose. Suddenly the city that had given me the best years of my life seemed tired and blowsy. I could no longer see the view of the Divinity School lawn for the soot on the windows, or hear the birds of St. Ronan Street for the roar of traffic on Whitney Avenue. I began to feel as if something were cutting off my oxygen, as if the secondhand English ivy of what is called the Yale Community might yet ensnare us, as if we could still calcify, like a couple of its ersatz gargoyles, if we didn't get moving.

And so we beat our way free of New Haven's vines and began our journey to the Great Northwest.

Our covered wagon was a first-year model Mitsubishi van which we filled with luggage and pillows and a few items we'd forgotten to put in the movers' truck, including a totemic Hindu statuette that gazed out the window at the turnpike, startling passing drivers as we hurtled west.

Within a couple of days the van was littered with the detritus of highway travel: cardboard motel ice buckets and minimart soda cans; Laura Scudder variety snack packs; trash bags; Triple-A road bibles; frayed, misfolded maps; highway bingo boards; Life Saver wrappings; business cards from restaurants; catalogs; apple cores; peach pits; film canisters; books; pads; pencils; cassette tapes; pens; markers; crayons; Barbie doll accessories; Dungeons and Dragons manuals and dice; and rewrapped Sugar Daddys rolled in lint.

I had tried to sell the proposition to my son and daughter in the same terms as Debbie had sold it to me; this would be a great adventure, I kept telling them, an immersion in the splendors of the American nation. But every now and then I would glance at the rearview mirror and see my Yankee children staring out at the ever-stranger highwayscape, at the double-wides and the Winnebagos with satellite dishes, at lakes the size of oceans, at deserts and mountains, dust devils, and thunderheads, at reservation gift shops and chain saw sculptures and live bait vending machines, at vast fields of sunflowers, and farmers' ponds filled with pelicans, and rows of gigantic sprinklers fanning the crops with their cool blue plumes.

Casey, who could not yet read a map, had to rely on her dwindling, vestigial faith that her mom and dad knew where they were going and what they were doing, while Jake drowned out his doubts with his headphones. *This is going to be good for them,* I told myself as we drove through Idaho and Montana, but Jake wasn't so sure, even—or maybe especially—after he recorded the highest score on a video game in Miles City, Montana, outpointing all the country boys who'd preceded him. And I wasn't so sure either, when we stopped at a water park in Sweet Grass County, where we had to sign insurance waivers and the puddled, mossy walkways were littered with Band-Aids.

As bugs and bird dung stippled our windshield and grasshoppers crackled like twigs against our grille, the sky seemed to double and then triple in size above us, and the horizon stretched out all around like a spreading stain, as though we'd somehow crossed into another dimension in which the farther you traveled to somewhere the farther you still had to go to get there, world without end, amen.

It was in North Dakota or Idaho or maybe as late as Montana that my Yankee provincialism kicked back in with a vengeance. I think it was when we were seated at Margaret's Chat 'n' Chew, or maybe it was the Royal Fork Buffet, that a perplexity that had been nagging at me ever since we crossed into Indiana finally gathered itself into a question. For almost a thousand miles we'd been hurtling through little towns full of people pulling into driveways, toting groceries, stepping out of banks, and at last I had to ask out loud, "What are all these people *doing* out here?"

Up until that moment, middle-American towns had existed solely for polling purposes, or maybe for those heartland reports you get every four years on the network news, where they dress up some Harvard boy in a lot of denim and stand him in front of a Civil War monument so he can take the pulse of the nation for us.

I guess I knew that the country needed maybe a few thousand farmers and some more folks to staff the motels and Jiffy Marts along the highway, but what were all these *other* people doing out here? In places with names like Alma and Cleghorn and Strum there seemed to be electricians and homemakers and custom insulators and loan officers, all going about their business a thousand miles from New York, as though their lives made a difference to somebody.

It wasn't until we hit the Cascades, I think, that it occurred to me that I was about to become one of these people: a local, a rustic, an object of wonder to visiting easterners. I imagined a lot of flannel would work its way into my wardrobe, and I would develop a reproachful impatience with the news of the world.

Not for me the rancid gossip of the publishing world. Not for me the corruptions of *The New York Times*. No, sir. I would garden. I would putter. I would fish. And if my literary ambitions survived my transplantation, I might someday acquire a backhanded reputation as a regional writer with novels set in fisheries and logging towns populated by survivalists in long johns and toques, and sturdy, casseroling women in gray woolen socks.

"What's your all-fired hurry?" I might ask my busy brother when he called. "Why, you're three hours ahead of yourself."

Honk

I DON'T know if anyone still takes their cues from bumper stickers. I like to think I'm immune to them, but every now and then I have to wonder.

On the long drive from New Haven to Seattle I fell in behind a car on the outskirts of Milwaukee that had "Honk if you love Jesus" emblazoned like a Band-Aid across its backside. I'd seen this sticker and its cousins often enough before—*Honk if you love whales, Honk if you love your secretary*—but somehow, in rush hour traffic, halfway between one home and another, I couldn't shake this one loose, and I began to consider its invitation to declare not only *my* fellowship with Jesus but my car's.

The stickered car in front of me looked battered and rangy, like a belligerent drunk staggering along a bar rail, and I began to wonder what other beliefs I might embrace if I gave my horn a Christian toot. Nonetheless, I decided I did love Jesus in my fashion, and here, after all, was a fellow human being reaching out to me, here on a strange road in an ever-stranger land. Maybe this move of ours was going to require that we accept such invitations, at least until we got our feet on the ground.

So, as I pulled into the lane beside him, I smiled beatifically and sang unto the Lord with a mighty honk.

The other driver, a livid, beefy man with a flat-top haircut, scowled at me for a few yards, stuck his arm out his window, and tossed me the bone.

I still don't know what his problem was. My wife figures that he thought we were making fun of him, or that he may have been in the middle of some kind of lapse, one of those spiritual troughs we all fall into now and then. But I have to figure it was probably just a secondhand car.

Crops

I HAVE a brief proposal to make to our nation's highway system, and then I'll be on my way. It seems to me that the time has come for farmers to caption their crops.

By the time my family and I had crossed the United States, we were sick to death of ignorantly speculating about the crops growing along our highways. You can buy field guides to just about anything in this country—shorebirds, seashells, wildflowers, rocks—just about anything but fields. What the farmers of this country don't seem to realize is that the rest of us don't know an alfalfa field from a golf course, and I don't see what the point is of growing all this stuff if the rest of us don't even know what it is.

Somewhere in the vicinity of Coeur d'Alene, Idaho, my family and I passed rows and rows of some kind of light blue firlike stuff that still has us completely buffaloed. There were whole families of people picking things off it, and rows of trucks waiting nearby to haul whatever it was away. I finally decided that it was those little berries they use to flavor gin, but then I don't know the name of them either, and it seems to me a long shot that they'd grow something like gin berries in Idaho.

My wife and I almost came to blows over artichokes. A field of elephant garlic nearly forced us off the road one time, and a couple of hundred acres of sugar beets beat the hell out of us for the better part of a day. I don't know how many city slickers have drifted off the road with their wits muddled by brussel sprouts, how many truckers have been driven to distraction by the enigma of broccoli—but if we're going to pass ourselves off as an informed electorate, I think the farmers of America had better start putting up some signs.

I know a lot of you think there are enough signs on the highway already, by which I suppose you mean billboards, but these don't have to be big and they don't have to be fancy. They could be small and low, like the old Burma-Shave signs, but readable at fifty paces and sixty-five miles an hour.

We're not talking here about government-issue road signs either. We're talking about homespun jobs, custom-made, with a nice little welcoming ring.

"You're looking at yellow mustard," maybe.

Or, "This here is rutabagas."

Or, "Will you look at Walter's new potatoes!"

Dashboards and Dragons

W*ITH* over three thousand miles of superhighway ahead of us I figured the best way to keep the kids entertained on our journey across the country was to buy them each a Walkman. That way their mother and I could chat and listen on the dashboard stereo while Casey and Jake silently nodded their headphoned heads to the thump and whine of Madonna and Twisted Sister.

But when four fiercely autonomous human beings are locked and belted into each other's company for eight, nine, ten hours a day, day after day, with no escape short of opening a window and flinging themselves out onto the highway, even the best of intentions go up in smoke.

For it turned out that what I had introduced into our journey was not the sweet music that soothes the savage breast but a family game as corrosive and divisive as croquet.

The ground rules took hundreds of miles to develop, but in the end they were simple enough. The game requires at least four players: the Dashboard Master, the Arbiter, and at least two Walkpersons.

For the purposes of this exposition I shall cast myself in the role of Dashboard Master, but the role can redound to whoever drives the car. The Dashboard Master can choose whatever tape he wishes to play, his only limitation being, according to the rules, that he always play something no more than one other player wants to hear. As the driver he is prohibited by law from wearing headphones and so must listen instead to the dashboard stereo, which plays through four speakers, over which he insists on exclusive control.

A second player, called an Arbiter, has neither a Walkman nor any say over what tapes may be played on the dashboard stereo. She may, however, occasionally turn down the volume on the dashboard stereo in order to hear herself bellow back at the Walkpersons to remove their headphones so that they can hear what the Arbiter's been trying to tell them for the past six miles, which is to turn down their headphones or they'll hurt their ears.

Though the two Walkpersons are provided with tape players of equal quality, their tape collections must vary considerably, so that in order to keep from going insane one must occasionally borrow from the other. The borrower acquires two points for borrowing a tape without permission, with additional points for leaving it out on the floor, which must be littered, almost from the outset, with popcorn, rolling soda cans, and apple cores.

Each Walkperson must be equipped with safe headphones, the kind that do not fit over the ear but rest in the shell of the ear, not in order to spare their developing eardrums the dangerous compression of cupped headphones but so as to allow outside noise from the other players to intrude on their listening pleasure.

During the first few turns the Dashboard Master and the Arbiter chat amicably about the wonderful journey that lies ahead, while the Walkpersons listen contentedly on their separate headphones.

But as the conversation in the front seat dries up, and the enormity of the trip begins to sink in (on the cross-continental version this occurs somewhere around New Jersey or Nevada, depending on where you start), the Dashboard Master rolls the dice by choosing a tape and inserting it into the dashboard stereo.

Depending on the selection, all three of the other players may protest, and here the Dashboard Master will have a choice of either insisting on his authority, thus setting the tone for much of the bitterness that follows, or retreating entirely, in which case the game might as well be over. So if he is any kind of Dashboard Master at all, he will respond to the other players' protests by turning up the volume.

At first the Arbiter remains silent, for she has seen this before and likes to think she can wait it out. But the Walkpersons are not so forbearing, and complain that they can't hear their machines over the noise from the dashboard. It is this tension between speaker and headphone that lies at the heart of the game.

The Walkpersons demand that the Dashboard Master turn off the two speakers in the back, which he is obliged to do, unless, of course, there is something on his dashboard stereo that he believes everyone would benefit from hearing: readings from T. S. Eliot, for instance, or perhaps an especially telling figure from Brahms's Second Piano Concerto.

Either way, the Walkpersons are now required to complain that even with the rear speakers turned off they still can't hear their music, at which point the Dashboard Master will instruct them to turn up their headphones. Here, of course, he parts company with the Arbiter, who reminds him that she has just told the children to turn down their headphones so they won't hurt their ears.

"Why don't we all just turn off the music and talk?" she may brightly suggest at this point.

"We *are* talking," the Dashboard Master replies, turning up the volume some more. "We're talking about *this*."

Once they have succeeded in dividing the Dashboard Master from the Arbiter, one of the Walkpersons may manifest an interest in listening to the Dashboard Master's tape and ask that he turn it up in the back. Here the second Walkperson may protest generally, or demand that the tape be played only on the opposite side of the car. This seems reasonable to the Arbiter, despite the Dashboard Master's perfectly valid argument that by turning off the speakers on the second Walkperson's side of the car he will cut off the stereo track containing half of the dialogue or all of the woodwinds.

"But I can't hear anything on my tape if you play both speakers," the second Walkperson will complain as the Dashboard Master balances his channels.

"He said he can't hear anything on his tape," says the Arbiter, shouting over the noise.

"I heard him," says the Dashboard Master.

"Don't snap at me," says the Arbiter, reaching for the controls.

"Don't touch those controls," snaps the Dashboard Master.

"I'm turning off the stereo," says the Arbiter.

"Like hell you are," reasons the Dashboard Master.

And so on across the Great Plains, the mighty Rockies, to the tranquil waters of Puget Sound.

Rainier

SHE first hove into view on a morning in August 1987, after we'd cleared the badlands and wheat fields of western Washington and proceeded into the foothills of the Cascades.

"Isn't that Mount Rainier?" Debbie asked, and I glanced up from my map just as we turned a curve in the highway and a huge white bank of something slipped behind a stand of firs.

"No, no," I told her confidently, checking the map again. "Mount Rainier's at least a hundred miles away."

But then the highway curved back again, and now there was no doubt about it. She was a mountain, all right, or at least she was in the shape of a mountain. But she was too damn big for a mountain, or in any case an American mountain, for though we were driving through the Cascades, nothing in the neighborhood approached the scale of this Arctic apparition. Like her volcanic cousins Fuji and Kilimanjaro, Rainier seemed to rise out of nowhere, like a great whale sounding.

Everywhere I've lived I've felt as though I had to come to grips with something or other. In Cornwall, Connecticut, it was the Housatonic River, in whose rapids I finally immersed myself one summer. In New Haven, God help me, it was Yale. In the Great Northwest I have Puget Sound to contend with, and the Olympics, and the city of Seattle, of course. But the most imposing proposition in these parts is Mount Rainier.

Our new home on Bainbridge Island faces west, toward the Olympics, but only three miles down our road the shore hooks around Point White, and from a small beach at Lynwood Center I can face southeast and watch Rainier looming over a limb of Puget Sound called Rich Passage. (I don't, by the way, call Rainier "she" out of reflex but because from Bainbridge Island Rainier suggests a mother, with Little Tahoma, her small spur, tugging at her skirt behind her.)

A while ago she threw a golden shawl of clouds over her shoulders and set out for an evening with the full moon. But the next morning, as if to atone for this brash display, she was as reclusive as a Hindu widow, barely perceptible through the morning scrim.

So how do I come to terms with an entity that can come and go at her pleasure, that employs the clouds as her wardrobe, that still holds the sun captive hours after the rest of us are languishing in the shadows?

Not, I suspect, by climbing her. A few years ago, *Life* magazine ran a series of pictures of the human skin that had been taken with a camera attached to an electron microscope. The microscope revealed a Pandemonium of crags and defiles and hirsute jungles populated by ticks and nits and land crabs. No one could contemplate those pictures without a shudder and an itch, but the perspective they provided, except perhaps to formulators of medicated shampoos, was merely freakish.

As I puzzle over the joy and dread Mount Rainier engenders, I find the accounts of mountain climbers just as freakish and beside the point. No matter how many pictures you may show me of shaggy, frostbitten climbers poised at the peak, flashing their cold white teeth at the camera, Mount Rainier is not conquerable. On her icy flesh the mountaineers are negligible parasites, jabbing minutely with their picks and spikes.

I guess I was right to worry that if I moved to the Northwest a couple of my screws might come loose, because every time I look at Mount Rainier I can hear them rattle. She is the soul of the Northwest, or maybe the ghost of its soul, sometimes a spectral reproach for everything we've done to spoil her view, but always a celebration of the immensities.

That Bainbridge Island Attitude

MY wife tells me that when I move to a new place I give disproportionate weight to the most fleeting exchanges. I suppose she's right, but there isn't much I can do about it. A shrug from a gas station attendant or a nod from a waitress is enough to send me off on hours of fretful speculation.

My family and I hit the Northwest cold, and we didn't know what to expect in the way of a welcome: maybe some of the same born-again sunniness we've come to dread on our visits to California.

But we soon found that Washingtonians are not at all like Californians. In fact, they seem to distrust Californians in much the same way New Englanders distrust New Yorkers.

On my first day on the island I was waiting in line at the local market when the man ahead of me asked if the store would accept a San Diego check.

"San Diego, eh?" said the woman at the register.

"Yeah," said the man. "My family and I just moved up here."

"Really?" said the woman, squinting at his check. "I just hope you didn't bring any of that San Diego attitude with you."

"As a matter of fact," he said, straightening up a little, "that's why we've moved here—to get away from that San Diego attitude."

"That doesn't matter," said the checker. "A lot of you move out here to get away from that San Diego attitude, and you just wind up bringing that San Diego attitude with you."

I don't know what the San Diego attitude is, but the Bainbridge Island attitude is not to suffer strangers too gladly, unless, of course, you're a stranger yourself, which is to say someone who's lived here less than twenty-five years. Like New Englanders, northwesterners prefer to hold back a little, at least until you've demonstrated that you're not just another of those frail fools who move away after the first quarter-century of wet weather.

We got here in the middle of a drought, which meant that though the lawn was pretty much of a goner, thus sparing me the task of killing it myself, the days were spectacular. In the morning I would go out with my cereal bowl to the canes that flank our yard and pluck a few blackberries over my Special K. And I would think to myself that whoever wrote Genesis might have reconsidered the exile from Eden if he'd only sat on my porch one morning, eating blackberries and watching the far side of Port Orchard Channel blush in the rising light.

But Bainbridge Islanders don't trust good weather. It's as though the sun itself were just another interloper from San Diego, as though a reputation for bad weather were all that stands between the Northwest and the perdition of southern California. So, as soon as the rains and mists and fogs were back by popular demand, and the sun had been reduced to a bit player on the atmospheric stage, there was a new bounce in the island's step.

When I checked in again with the grocery clerk on a wet and windy January morning, suddenly she was all "How can I help you folks?" and "You come back soon" and "I know you're going to love your new home."

The Gazzam House

BAINBRIDGE ISLAND seemed to me amazingly un-spoiled for a suburb of Seattle until one afternoon in the spring of 1988 when I borrowed a neighbor's kayak and for the first time pulled my way up Port Orchard Channel.

I was top-heavy and a little ungainly with my dripping paddle, so I kept close enough to the beach to wade ashore in case I capsized. But the water was clear all the way down to the barnacled stones scattered along the bottom, and it was agreeable slipping north among the wigeons and pintails, cormorants and gulls.

The road that parallels the beach turns to gravel half a mile past my house and begins a treacherous climb back from the steep shoreline. So I always assumed that the houses had to leave off not much farther on, and that from the end of Crystal Springs a mile or so to Fletcher Bay I would find nothing but woods.

As I paddled along, however, I discovered that no measure of ingenuity was being spared to build homes along the water, and that the beach's steep clay flanks were crisscrossed with wooden stairs. Some of the houses were a few decades old, and from the neatly stacked cordwood, the rusting swing sets and peeling, overturned tender boats lying in weeds beyond the tide's reach, I supposed that the occupants were probably venerable.

But among these old homes brand-new houses are making architectural statements, sometimes at the top of their voices. Looming expanses of tinted glass, and vertical-plank designer siding, and pressure-treated gazebos, and Japanesey pool enclosures have displaced the wooded shore of my wistful assumptions. Great stretches of beach had already been spoken for, and I could hear the whine of skill saws and the reports of nail guns and the heavy thud of pilings being driven in for yet another lofty deck.

The house I bought is eighty-six years old, and seems sometimes to share my disdain for new construction. But in its time, which is to say turn-of-the-century, it was no less an intrusion than the disportments of architectural whimsy now frolicking along the shore. In fact, my house was the first of its scale on the southwestern coast of Bainbridge Island to impose itself on what had been a sparse and informal smattering of Indian encampments, truck farms, summer cottages, and millworkers' homes.

Some foggy mornings I pose on my deck like an explorer on a ship glimpsing a pristine, primordial world. But when the fog lifts, my view is punctuated by other houses, and my home testifies not to the island's permanence but to the rangy flimflam and wall-eyed hubris of its history.

My house was built in 1905 by a real estate speculator and honorary Alabama colonel named Warren Lea Gazzam, who dreamed of turning the Bainbridge side of Port Orchard Channel into a Millionaire's Row. In order to make his holdings accessible to commuters he cofounded a ferry line called the Kitsap Transportation Company, and it is as its president that the island still remembers him.

Nicknamed the "White Collar Line" both for its highfalutin airs and for the distinctive white stripe on its smokestacks, the K.T.C.'s mosquito fleet ferried passengers and produce up and down the sound for almost a quarter of a century. From Tacoma to Seattle the K.T.C. and its competitors vied for dominance like opposing navies. Warfare extended beyond routes and rates to lawsuits, fistfights, races, and rammings, and provided Puget Sound not only with its primary form of transportation but with a glorious year-round spectator sport, until the construction of a few strategic bridges, the advent of the automobile, and the ravages of the Great Depression brought the game to a close.

I've been trying to pin down a few facts about the Colonel and his business ventures, but they are hard to come by. His influence, not to say his generosity, seems to have compromised a lot of the local newspaper accounts of his enterprises. Their stories are full of those exchanges that occur only in fully paid-for Edwardian booster journalism, in which the poor outclassed oaf who presumes to compete with the Colonel compounds his greed with cursing and bad grammar, whereas our hero coolly disguises his rapacity in the flag, fair play, and the mantle of Progress, without so much as dangling a participle.

The son of a prominent but impecunious family in Mobile, Alabama, Warren Gazzam suffered from tuberculosis as a young man and was sent to recuperate in Arizona, where, as an Indian agent, he collected tribal artifacts and was witness to the surrender of Geronimo. The West seemed to suit his entrepreneurial bent, and he proceeded to Seattle, where he opened a notions shop on Second Avenue. With his aristocratic southern flourish the Colonel insinuated himself into

Seattle high society, and at a time when men in the Northwest outnumbered women ten to one, he summoned and successfully married off all three of his sisters to men of substance.

For his own spouse he chose Lizzie Lulu Yeaton, the daughter of a Baptist pioneer from New Hampshire and the first white female to be born in Spokane, Washington—whom the Colonel presumed to be well-to-do when he first spotted her arriving at his shop in a carriage. Though the marriage produced four children, it was not a success. On their wedding night the Colonel is said to have announced to his devout young bride that as a southern gentleman he could not be expected to be faithful, and indeed he rose to this diminished expectation all his life, and had the honor of being named as a corespondent in a divorce when he was ninety-one years old.

From the start the Colonel proved an erratic provider, his speculations sometimes taking precedence over the exigencies of fatherhood. Even as he slapped the backs of his wealthy brethren at the Rainier Club in Seattle, the family was sometimes hard put to set food upon its table, and then the Colonel would breeze in and present his wife with a diamond necklace or announce he had purchased a steamboat company.

So when a local architect named William Alberts was commissioned in 1903 to design a summer house for the Gazzams on Bainbridge Island, he had to accommodate not only the Colonel's pretensions but Mrs. Gazzam's austerity and the local scarcity of master craftsmen.

The result was a large but simple house of niggardly construction: six thousand square feet enclosed in fir studs and cedar shakes and walls of native stone. What the Colonel dubbed "Alabama," but shall always be known as the Gazzam House, was to be the first of many mansions he envisioned dotting the shoreline, albeit at discreet distances from one another.

He assured his own privacy by the sheer dimensions of his surrounding estate: five hundred acres of beach and orchard, forest and lake, and freshly cleared meadowland. The house was so remote, in fact, that until Mrs. Gazzam opened a post office of her own in the back hall, she had to row a mile across the channel to Illahee every day to pick up the mail.

All but abandoned by her restless husband, Mrs. Gazzam turned for strength to Mary Baker Eddy, and "Alabama" became a gathering place for Mrs. Gazzam's fellow Christian Scientists, who would arrive aboard the K.T.C.'s ferries at Crystal Springs Landing and climb the stone stairway to the house for colloquies and luncheons.

Under the tutelage of one of Warren's sisters, who lived in an area of the island known as the Country Club, the Colonel's three daughters were introduced to the rigors of what locally passed for high society, and the downstairs of the house, with its sixty feet of floor space from living room hearth to dining room window, became the island's premier ballroom.

The Colonel rarely visited his own estate, and took up residence, when he was not traveling, across the channel in Bremerton. But for Gazzam's son and three daughters, and for many of the children in its vicinity, the estate acquired an almost mystical significance. After gathering blackberries along its trails, harvesting pears and apples in its orchards, digging for clams on its beaches, fishing for lingcod and black-mouth salmon off its pier, reading books on its window seats in the drizzling light of a winter afternoon, they would bear the abiding imprint of its landscape all the rest of their lives.

The Colonel's ties to his family were never strong, and they were finally broken in the 1920s when he blamed Lulu's attachment to the Mother Church (and she, in turn, blamed his skepticism) for the death, from meningitis, of his youngest child and namesake: a brilliant, congenial boy who had constructed the island's first radio while still in his teens.

But there had been other irregularities along the way. The Colonel's household had once included a young woman named Madge, only five years his oldest daughter's senior, whose medical education he generously financed even after Lulu finally evicted her out of a less than farfetched suspicion that she was dallying with her husband.

After their divorce the Colonel gave Lulu the run of the Bainbridge Island house. Lea, her oldest daughter, was a dynamo and Mary a great beauty, and the Colonel sent them both to college. But the second daughter, Ruth, had been so frail as a small child that she had not been expected to live, and, fearing for her health and perhaps overextended by Madge's tuition, the Colonel announced that he would not send Ruth to college but to New York for a year of refinement under the wing of another of his socialite sisters.

Eventually all three daughters—Lea, Ruth, and Mary—married and moved away. Ruth married Pierce Haight, the son of the tyrant of a prominent Seattle law firm who denied Pierce his ambition to teach history and demanded that he become an attorney. Unprepared by his genteel upbringing for the harsh exigencies of corporate law, Pierce primarily depended for his livelihood on income from his share of the family fortune. When he lost his home and most of his fortune to the Depression, Lulu invited Ruth and her family to live with her at "Alabama," to which Ruth agreed only on condition that she earn her family's keep running the house as a summer hotel.

And so in the late spring of 1934 the family moved into the barn and opened the Gazzam House, as it was now officially dubbed, to summer boarders seeking, according to the brochure, "a quiet, truly restful place to spend a vacation."

The grounds still included a lake, miles of trails, and, of course, the beach, which, the northwestern climate being what it is, could offer only "a chance" for sunbaths.

The waitresses who tended to the summer guests at the huge table in the dining room were University of Washington students who lived in tents in a nearby meadow. But the major feature of a stay at the Gazzam House was evidently the cooking of "Black Bertha," as the family called her, who won "the hearts of all at Gazzam house in the traditional southern manner." The house owed its "adequate" heat to a series of men who lived in the cellar and stoked the furnace with cordwood cut from the surrounding estate.

Innkeeping did not suit Lulu Gazzam for long, and she eventually moved to the University of Washington, where she worked for the rest of her life as a sorority housemother. But Ruth proved a gifted hostess, and word of the Gazzam House spread quickly among Seattle's travel agents. For the next five summers Ruth Haight filled every room with vacationers—mostly from Seattle but a few from California, Minnesota, and even New York—lured by the low rates, good food, charming location, and rounds of bridge with the courtly and erudite Mr. Haight in the parlor.

On one of his birthdays the Colonel's intermittently estranged family presented him with a confection in the shape of his property. But when he was asked to cut the first slice, he ordered the cake returned to the kitchen, declaring that he had never subdivided his holdings and wasn't about to start now.

Nevertheless, when his speculations backfired in the chill of the Great Depression, he began to shed his property. As the Depression ground on, the Colonel, reduced by now to running a small hotel in Bremerton, didn't keep up his "Alabama" payments to the bank, and one day in 1938 Ruth's children returned from school to find a foreclosure notice on the door.* And so Ruth Gazzam Haight and her family moved to a small house on a cliff overlooking Manitou Beach, from which she commuted to work for her father and where she and her family subsisted, for a time, on clams.

The bank subdivided the estate, clearing the way for an access road by tearing down the stone staircase that once led from the front porch to the orchards along the beach, and sold "Alabama" to a bachelor florist named Charlie Sullivan. Sullivan studded the grounds with five thousand camellia bushes and installed a chromium kitchen that was a horror to his predecessors. After fifty years of motley ownership and sporadic occupation the property shrank to a single acre, the orchard made way for a string of cottages, and all but a dozen of Sullivan's camellias died in a freeze in the 1950s.

Those of us whose imaginations and savings have been caught up in the old Gazzam House have been, all in all, as hapless as the Colonel himself. Though its squandered estate is even now being nibbled up by other less romantic developers, its grandiosity remains contagious.

The house is shot through with visionary wiring concepts in varying states of incompletion, beginning with Gazzam's own tangle of knob-and-tube he installed long before this end of the island had even been electrified. (He once attempted, without success, to generate power in the feeble trickle from a nearby spring.) Sometimes, as I fumble with the eight kitchen light switches, it seems as though the house has been wired by the Marx Brothers. Three-prong wall sock-

---

* It was Warren Gazzam's lifelong ambition to die a millionaire, and when World War II filled his Bremerton hotel with visitors to the shipyard, he thought he might finally become one. But he held out too long before selling the place, and when he died his assets seem to have amounted to only about four hundred thousand dollars. Nonetheless, he got his wish, after a fashion, by having had the foresight to bribe the editor of a local paper to headline his obituary COLORFUL MILLIONAIRE DIES.

ets have been directly connected to the ungrounded wiring from the Colonel's days, live bare sections of which, I soon discovered, jutted out into the birds' nests under the attic eaves.

One owner decided on a Saturday morning to hike up the sag in the living room floor. So, according to his son, he made his way into the crawl space with his car jack and happily began to pump away at a succession of joists, bracing them with cinder blocks. Everything seemed to be going great until he heard a toppling noise overhead and rushed up to find that all of the downstairs plaster had fallen off the walls.

The original dark fir woodwork survived the Sheetrocking that followed, though it didn't quite fit back in places over the slightly thickened surface of the walls. Most of the windows are the now-rippled originals, and a couple of panes in the living room are still perforated by the BBs the neighborhood kids shot at the Gazzams' ghosts during "Alabama's" various phases of abandonment. The attic rafters bear the scorched traces of a fire, and the upstairs floorboards have the raised grain of wood once exposed to rain.

Replacing the plaster in the master bedroom, I have come upon widely separated one-by-four studs that do not reach the rafters, rafters that do not connect to wall plates, floating wall plates butted up against the ends of joists—as if perhaps during the house's construction the masonry cost more than the Colonel had expected, or halfway through he suffered one of his reversals and asked the boys with a nudge and a wink to go easy on the materials.

All these things give the house resonance, as though by possessing it I have come to share in its hapless ancestry. As I make my own minor and trepidatious alterations, I experience a nagging anxiety that the house will defeat me just as it seems to have defeated all my predecessors, that it is coaxing me ever closer to the edge of its own shifting precipice.

"Alabama's" feet are clay, and some years before we arrived

here the front yard collapsed in a rainstorm, burying the little road that feeds the driveways below. So my immediate predecessor had to shave off the steepest angle of the ledge, and jam road-grade material into its slope to hold it fast, and lay a curtain drain that now piddles rainwater all the way down to the channel. But the body of the island keeps trying to reject this monument to Gazzam's transplanted aspirations. Now new fissures are beginning to open up here and there which I must fill with sand, and grass won't grow in the tamped, rocky clay.

The Gazzam House, in its apparent solidity, seems to evoke a continuity that eludes all of us who live here and reproaches us for our fecklessness. But like the newest structures rising along the shore it's an imposition on this primeval island that's sustained only by the continual sinking of pipes and posts and footings. Viewed from a bird's-eye vantage, Warren Lea Gazzam's "Alabama" is no less an artifice for the stand of hundred-year-old firs and cedars that surrounds it on three sides, no less a detriment to the wilderness for its native anatomy of fir and cedar and stone, no less an intrusion for its flea market claims to antiquity.

But its grip on the sensibilities of its owners seems everlasting. Time after time we will glance out one of its windows to see a car pausing in the driveway, its occupants gazing up with a yearning and regret that is unmistakably nostalgic. Sometimes I wave to them or call out to them to invite them in, but usually they decline and hurry off instead, as if pained to see the house occupied by anyone but their own lingering ghosts.

One July morning in 1988 I got a call from the president of the local historical society, who said that a Gazzam descendant was visiting the island and would like to see the house. So I rushed around to clear the place of my family's detritus and stepped out into the driveway to greet none other than Ruth Gazzam Haight herself, still thriving, thank you very much, at ninety-four years of age.

Had I been looking for a surrogate grandmother in the Great Northwest, Ruth Haight would have fit the bill. Silver-haired and sprightly, she wore a blue floral dress and the requisite pearls, and stood in the front yard with her niece Barbara and her sons, Warren and Gil, shielding her eyes from the sun and asking, Where had the orchard disappeared to? When had all these huge evergreens around the house sprung up? What had become of the rest of the deck?

And then before anyone could answer her she caught sight of me, took my hand in both of hers, and declared how delighted she was that a family was living in her girlhood home again; that it was, as she presumed, a happy house.

She was surprised to see how close the water now appeared from the yard, for in the old days the orchard had blocked the view of the shore. Did I know, she wondered, that the house had been built from stones gathered along the beach? I had speculated about that, I told her, because it would explain why for a hundred yards north and south of the house there are no large rocks left along the shore, and why the thousands of otherwise smooth stones that protrude from the first-story walls like baked rolls from a muffin tin bear the floury traces of barnacles and periwinkles.

And did she know, I asked her, that she had acquired a leading role in my daughter's imagination? Casey and her friends sometimes pretended to be the Gazzam girls as they explored the house and beach.

"But how could they ever have known about us?" she wanted to know.

"Step this way," I said, and led her around to the side of the house where Casey had found Ruth's and her siblings' names scratched into the cement of the foundation. Ruth said she remembered the day they wrote their names; it had been a warm summer day, the foundation had just been poured, and she and her family were living in a little beach house down the road. Peering along the wall, she identified a mysterious "W" as the initial of Warren junior, her dead brother. When she moved into the house, she told me, she was, like Casey, nine years old.

Her eyes teared up when she crossed the threshold; everything looked very much as it had when she and her family left the house fifty years before. The Arthurian table, chairs, and sideboard her father had commissioned for the house in 1905 still occupied the dining room, and for a moment one of her sons wondered if we hadn't gotten hold of their old china as well.

"Remember," Gil asked his brother Warren, pointing up to a Quimper plate on the china shelf along the ceiling, "how insulted I used to be if I finished my soup and there was a lady on the bottom of my bowl?"

And then he paused and peered at me in astonishment. "But where did you get my grandfather's china?"

It was actually *my* grandfather's china, and this was only the first of a series of coincidences and affinities to emerge during Ruth's visit. Puzzled by a display shelf along the hallway walls, my wife had decided to line it with Indian baskets (until she discovered what they cost). Ruth said that in fact her father had one of the largest collections of Indian baskets in the Northwest and had displayed them not only on the hallway shelves but on the living room settle as well. And the Japanese woodcuts we had recently inherited and which now hung in our dining room turned out to be very much like the Japanese woodcuts that once adorned the dining room walls in Mrs. Gazzam's time.

Mrs. Gazzam's woodcuts had come from a Japanese neighbor named Furuya, who, according to the xenophobic laws of the period, was not allowed as a first-generation Japanese immigrant to own land. The Colonel agreed to hold Furuya's property for him in his name, and for this Mr. Furuya, a prosperous importer and later the Japanese consul in Seattle, lavished gifts upon the Gazzams: a suite of teak furniture for the library, grass paper for the downstairs walls (which peeled off the night after it was first applied), and an elaborate screen for the dining room which so offended Mrs. Gazzam's taste that she had the reverse side papered over and would turn it face forward only when she heard the crunch of Mrs. Furuya's wooden sandals approaching up the driveway.

Ruth was married in front of the living room's stone fireplace, which the family festooned with flowers. An upright piano her grandmother Yeaton had brought by covered wagon from New Hampshire had stood where my grandfather's piano now stood, and back in the thirties Ruth had hired Ivan Novikoff (or "Ivan Awful Cough," as Ruth's husband called him), an eye-patched Russian dancing master, to teach the girls and boys of Bainbridge Island the fox-trot, the box step, and the Lambeth walk.

According to Ruth's sons, the Japanese used to do a lot of fishing in front of the house, and out in the channel the boys had once caught a lingcod of such proportions that it took both of them to wrestle it up to the house. I reported to them about the cutthroat trout I'd caught from my lawn, and everyone listened politely.

So Ruth Gazzam Haight had not only survived the Depression and the Colonel and the loss of her beloved "Alabama"; she and her family had thrived. After his father died in the late 1940s, Pierce Haight found his footing as the senior partner of his own law firm and before his death in 1967 fulfilled his lifelong pedagogic ambition by teaching history at the Bush School in Seattle, where Ruth, employing the administrative skills she developed as hostess of the Gazzam House, ran the residential program.

Escaping from Manitou Beach in 1939, her son Gil worked his way through Stanford University, acquired a Rhodes Scholarship, and went on to a distinguished career as a professor of chemistry; his sister, Mary, a graduate of Smith, married a professor of history and is now one of the Bush School's most celebrated teachers; and their brother Warren became a businessman of substance and consequence in Hawaii.

I don't know if, like the snail, we transport our houses with us, if their atmospheres cling to us in layers like a shell. But my family haunts all its houses in its dreams. My grandfather died in the sprawling house he built from a little cottage in Ohio and inhabited for sixty years, and I think my father may choose to die in the drafts of the old mansard house he and my mother have occupied for twenty-five years, and maybe I, too, have found my resting place, in Warren Lea Gazzam's one enduring fancy.

"We would still be here, you know," Ruth confided as we finally said goodbye. "If it hadn't been for my father's speculations, we would never have left this place."

"I know," I said.

And then I told her about the first time I toured the house the year before, in the company of a Realtor, a week after I'd first glimpsed it through the bushes.

"Well, Andy, I've got a few more houses to show you," he said as I lingered in the hallway. "So maybe we'd better move along."

"No," I told him, sitting on the stair. "You don't understand. I want *this* house. This is my house."

Dogs in the Road

A WOMAN wrote to the local paper here to report that a hit-and-run artist had killed her dog and left her small son to contend with the carnage. She decried all the reckless drivers who come careening along our twisting country lanes without giving a thought to the dogs that have roamed the island since long before the internal combustion engine.

But then a second woman wrote back the next week to suggest that the fault lay not in our cars but in ourselves. As far as she was concerned, it was high time local dog owners kept their pets out of harm's way: on leashes, at least, or preferably penned up in their yards.

My own dogs don't like the out-of-doors and stick close to the hearth. Nevertheless, the time has come for me to take a stand on the loose-dog issue, for the keeping of dogs seems to be a key to the distinction between the suburbs and the country.

When I first laid eyes on Bainbridge Island, I had just spent the day out in the better enclaves of Seattle's immediate suburbs, looking for a house in which to sink the shameful profit we thought we were going to make on the sale of our house in Connecticut. I drove through dozens of gated, dry-cleaned compounds, with yards so tidy they could have been trimmed by barbers. I never saw a child who hadn't been segregated into a rec room, or a dog that hadn't been penned or chained or kept indoors.

But on Bainbridge Island there were tricycles on the porches, and tufts of high grass under the fence rails where the lawn mower hadn't reached. And most of all there were dogs everywhere: casual interminglings of retrievers and setters scratching themselves by the roadsides, dozing on the dividing lines, barking from the decks.

The island is only half an hour's ferry ride from Seattle, and a huge proportion of people, my wife included, are commuters. So for all practical purposes we are suburbanites, except for a few agrarian holdouts who still raise things for a living—strawberries, raspberries, grapes.

Most islanders seem to think that the ferry is the island's salvation, that the crossing is a kind of thresher that separates those commuters who volunteer to live here because they have an affinity for it from those who might otherwise land here by default. And in fact, the ferry crossing that the commuters must make to get to work seems to have prevented Bainbridge Island, at least for the time being, from taking on the suburban aspect of Mercer Island and Bellevue, which are linked to Seattle by bridges.

I don't know what it is in us that so abhors a suburb. Maybe it's the feeling that security and proximity to shopping malls do not a hometown make. We realize too late that whenever we contrive to make it more convenient for us to spend our money we've made it at least as convenient for somebody else to take our money, and we wind up with communities that are neither here nor there.

I suppose people shouldn't expose their dogs to the pedestrian hazards of the machine age just to preserve the illusion that we live in the country. But the dogs are islanders too, and I would miss their dopey greetings as I pass them on the road. Like tarmac, like speed bumps, like security guards at the gate, a leash law would inch us toward suburbia, with a bridge to the city not very far behind.

The Visitor

OUR house came with a battered old rowboat, and after entertaining a sales pitch at the hardware store I bought myself a crab pot with which to trap the aristocratic Dungeness crabs that the Realtor told us we'd find in such abundance off our beach. So one morning in October I rowed out to what I guessed to be a depth of fifty feet and dropped my square crab pot into the tide.

The pot was a mesh box with several one-way doors through which the crabs were supposed to sample the bait: a wire-bound moldering chicken that had begun to assert itself from the rear of our new refrigerator.

I've since read that I shouldn't have bought a square pot but a round one, because crabs are literal-minded. When they catch the scent of the bait, they will follow the circular wall of a round crab pot until they've fumbled through the trapdoor. But if they must scrabble along the straight side of a square pot, they will often neglect to turn the corner and may continue instead along a straight course for yards and yards beyond the trap, never to return.

And yet it was with high hopes that Casey and I went out in our rowboat that evening to collect our catch. The channel was still as I rowed us up to the pot float, and we could hear fish slapping at the surface hundreds of feet away. I hauled up the trap line hand over hand to find that the chicken was gone, bones and all, and that the one crab I'd managed to inconvenience was now perched atop my pot, only to hop off its elevator ride just as it neared the surface. Casey and I watched it descend with its claws outstretched like an armored bird of prey, spiraling downward through a constellation of jellyfish.

Anyway, the crabbing was a bust, but Casey seemed unconcerned, and despite her early day-care training in the handling of live crustaceans, I think she may have been a little relieved that we weren't going to have to touch the things. She sat at her end of the rowboat with a dreamy look, and no wonder, for as the sun cruised down behind the Olympics, it was erecting a canopy of saffron clouds.

We talked for a while about how we'd landed on our feet out here in the Great Northwest; how with a blind roll of the dice we'd come up with a resonant old house, a good school with good teachers and even a nice bus driver. In fact, Casey and I were feeling so smug that we almost failed to notice a third head emerging to my right and peering up at us with a twitch of its dripping whiskers.

Our visitor was a young sea lion that had probably followed an errant salmon or a school of herring into the channel. At a profound loss for words we stared back into his mild black eyes until he seemed discomfited and followed his nose into the deep with an eloquent plunk and gurgle.

Although it's hard to tell when a sea lion is cavorting and when it's feeding, I think this one cavorted, rising and then disappearing for thirty seconds, a minute, two minutes, before reappearing impossible distances from where he'd last surfaced, snorting and turning his head toward us as if to make sure we were still watching.

"You know, Dad," Casey said as we rowed home. "Sometimes I can't believe I am who I am."

Drew

My son, Jake, isn't given to looking on the bright side of things, but back when we were driving toward this vague destination we'd proposed called Bainbridge Island, Washington, he announced he was going to make a fresh start out here. He wasn't going to lie about what he'd been back in New Haven, he said, but he wasn't going to volunteer anything about it either.

I didn't tell Jake what little stock I put in resolutions, for in this regard Jake was already five years ahead of where his father was at his age. It wasn't until I was eighteen that I tried to re-create myself. I hadn't had much luck with girls in high school, so when I went off to college I decided I was going to make myself over completely. I would dress in a lot of tweed, affect a scarf, smoke Camels, and read French existentialists in the snack bar.

But first I was going to have to dispose of the name "Andy." Andy seemed to me a sidekick's nickname, a salesman's handle: kind of feckless and happy-go-lucky. So I opted instead for "Drew." Drew was a variation on Andrew that seemed to me unique, exotic, and bright with promise, and I imagined flocks of turbulent girls—thespians, political scientists, studio art majors—comparing notes about him.

"Oh God, that Drew. Drew can be such a bastard, but he's—he's so great."

So I got Drew a herringbone sports jacket and a wool scarf and a copy of *L'Etranger* and led him off to college. But Drew turned out to be even more of a coward than Andy, for when a dark-eyed girl in a Gypsy skirt introduced herself during freshman orientation, Drew lost all his color and choked on his name, and good old Andy had to cover for him.

I'm glad I didn't tell Jake about Drew, because my son actually managed to pull off his transformation. I don't know what did the trick—Jake's will, or maybe his wardrobe, or puberty most likely—but two months later I overheard him breaking up gently but firmly with the third in a continuing string of girlfriends.

"I'm crying, Jake," she told him. "Okay? Are you happy?"

"I'm sorry you're feeling bad, Carol," I heard him tell her. "But I'm not going to cave in to emotional blackmail."

Which actually puts Jake more like *forty* years ahead of his old man.

Ralph

BY the time Debbie and I moved here our two dogs were elderly, and showing it. Ralph and Dolores were both deaf and blind, and Ralph was so weak in the hind legs that he walked on his pasterns and had to be carried up stairs.

And he was incontinent. For six months I'd followed after him with scoopers and paper towels, scrub brushes and rug shampoo, until finally at supper one evening he announced with a turd by my daughter's dining chair that it was time to say goodbye. So my wife and I made an appointment at the vet and drove old Ralphie to his doom.

Eighteen years ago Debbie and I had decided that our marriage had boiled down to a choice between a trial separation and getting a pet. So we went to the pound one Saturday and selected a secondhand dachshund named Linda.

Like all hounds Linda was a wanderer, and she wandered into the embrace of a standard poodle and produced six black puppies. We gave four away, but we decided to keep Ralph, the lone male, and when we got down to it we decided we couldn't part with Dolores, either. She was the runt of the litter, a doe-eyed dog with ears that trailed along beside her as she loped apologetically among her siblings. Ralph was the hairiest of the lot, long of fuselage like his mother but otherwise a fun-house mirror image of Dolores, with a baggy-pantsed gait and judiciary sprays of eyebrow.

Debbie and I eventually decided to blame the suburbs for our difficulties and moved without prospect to eight acres in the country. Within a couple of years Linda had vanished on one of her safaris into the popple swamp across the road, but Ralph and Dolores flourished, rooting through the meadow above our house, sleeping in straw in the horse barn.

Debbie and I also found our footing in the country, and with it we acquired ambitions that led us into the city of New Haven, where Ralph and Dolores resigned themselves to leashes and traffic and the clumsy affections of two toddlers. They became sociable city dogs, and what they did for eight years to the little strip of Yale across the street from our house was no worse than what Yale had been doing to the rest of the city for almost three centuries.

I wrote to the song of their snoring, raised my children under their scrutiny, and everywhere I went in the apartments and houses of my fatherhood they followed, alert to crumbs and milk spills and the mailman's tread. They never asked me for a lot of attention because they had each other. For seventeen years they groomed each other and shared each other's dishes and kept each other warm in the night drafts.

When the time came to move west it was a toss-up whether we would spring for their air freight or put them down. Dolores saved them both, at least for a little while. She was just as deaf and blind as her brother, but she was still continent and spry, and we could neither cut her off in her golden years nor separate her from her brother, for the two of them together were as symmetrical and complementary as bookends.

So a friend of ours cared for them as we drove across the country, and on a weekday morning two months later they arrived at Sea-Tac airport in gray plastic kennels. I tried to talk up our new home as I washed them off on the Bainbridge

Island ferry. I guess I'd hoped they might perk up out here, chasing the rabbits out of the garden and tilting their noses in the breeze from the channel.

But they were too old and tired and citified to devote themselves to my romantic notions of renewal and continuity. *You may fly us three thousand miles to live among the mountains,* they seemed to grumble as we let them out to pee. *But life is earnest and bounded, and ours is drawing to a close.*

Ralph didn't rage against the dying of the light, exactly, but he jumped so when the vet probed for his vein that he broke her hypodermic, and as she hurried off to get another vial of anesthesia he peered up at me with a betrayed look.

Ralph had been born in my presence and now he was dying in my arms, and I was just a shadow to him, looming in the fluorescent glare.

"I know, old buddy," I said. "I know."

But I didn't know, and I still don't know, what becomes of an old dog's soul.

Silver and Gold

I HAVE always subscribed to the notion that if you get too open-minded your brains fall out. But I suppose that if I'm to make any friends out here at all, I'm at least going to have to leave the door ajar.

Our East Coast friends who came to visit liked our new-found home so much that we thought we might be able to make an end run around the friendship search and merely colonize the island with old buddies, tried and true. But as soon as they get home our old friends seem to get a grip on themselves, and it's apparent that despite our departure they still insist on leading lives of their own, no matter how many salmon we may grill for them or real estate listings we may send after them in the mail.

So there's no help for it; we need new friends. And out of this need I have had to learn to withhold judgment on people, a deprivation that causes me almost physical distress. I can no longer afford to assume, from the severity of a man's haircut, that he signs over his dividend checks to the fund for Oliver North, nor can I determine from the plaid of his sports jacket that he's in sales, because out here there doesn't seem to be any dress code, and he could just as easily be a nurse practitioner who shares my enthusiasm for Mario

Cuomo, the history of African exploration, and the early works of Bruce Jay Friedman.

I sometimes wish that I could see movies of my first meetings with people who were later to become my oldest and dearest friends. Perhaps by reviewing our initial pleasantries and posturings I could find some harbinger of what it was that finally clicked, and devise a kind of catalog of cues, a social early warning system, with which I could now distinguish good leads from bum steers as I search for buddies in the Great Northwest.

Naturally enough, I began my search close to home, among the welcoming ranks of our new neighbors. We've had great luck in our choice of neighbors, and indeed by the end of my first week I knew more of my neighbors here than I ever knew after nine years in one house in New Haven. As soon as we showed up, people came by with bouquets and baskets of home-canned and home-baked goods, and invitations to drop by for burgers and cocktails out by the beach.

But I think I sometimes brought too much to bear on my first encounters with the folks on my street, and they backed off a few steps from my lonely ardor. I gripped their hands a little too long, nodded a little too eagerly at their small talk, and as we grinned at each other I kept searching their faces for some hint of the relationship to come. Would we visit each other's decks and exchange confidences on the vagaries of existence, or would we soon be glowering at each other over the thorn rows of blackberry and excoriating each other in front of the zoning commission?

The Yankee in me is afraid that neighbors, by definition, are too intimate a part of your life to be the best of friends. Friendship is too fragile to withstand a steady barrage of overturned garbage pails and misfiring burglar alarm systems. By cultivating friendship with a neighbor, you lose, for what it's worth, the flexibility of mere acquaintanceship and thus deny yourself the satisfaction and high drama of neighborly wrath and outrage over badly parked cars, errant hardballs, and baying, insomniac dogs.

My wife and kids have had better luck finding friends beyond the edge of Crystal Springs Beach. I like to think it's because they all spend their day at school, and school, be it graduate or primary, is basically a social institution, whereas writing is hermetic. Writers don't generate friends any more readily than they generate income, so I think if I do manage to make a lasting friend or two, it's going to be one of my wife's colleagues, or one of the parents of my children's friends, a generous fellow of complementary enthusiasms who can see past my yanking handshake and my aimless chit-chat to a homesick man in search of a pal.

Bum Fish

AFTER a couple of months of watching the fish slap at the surface of the channel off our beach, I finally drove to the hardware store to buy myself a rod and reel. And a license, of course, and line, and bait and hooks and weights and floats and spoons and leads and swivels.

The tide was in by the time I got home, and I headed down to the little patch of beachside yard that came with the house and stood on the concrete floodwall and cast a spoon out into the tide, displacing for a while the little flock of wigeons that winters in these waters.

As a boy I used to fish with worms and floats, and though I never caught anything but sunfish, the technique was simple and the results were sure. But casting a spoon is another matter. You're supposed to jerk it slightly as you reel it in so that it impersonates a wounded fish, flashing seductively as it limps through the water. But there are a lot of variables: where you cast, with what impact the spoon hits the water, how long you should wait and thus how deep the spoon should sink before you start reeling it in, how fast you should reel it in, how hard you should jerk on the line, and so on. Weighing these factors and contemplating their permutations, I find that my faith, which has always been pretty shaky, starts to falter and a whine arises from somewhere back in my boyhood. "Oh, what's the use. I'm *never* going to catch a fish."

A couple of doors down the beach lives Mr. Eagen, an alert and elderly neighbor who grew up on the island and takes a dim and mordant view of newcomers.

"Whatcha doin'?" he asked, walking to the corner of his yard.

"Oh, just doing a little fishing," I said with an abashed nod.

"Well, you know, Andy," he said, lifting his ball cap, "I just gotta tell ya. I don't know how they fish back East, but that's not how we catch fish out here."

Defeat and humiliation are a man's daily diet in this life, but every now and then he is apportioned a moment of pure and exquisite victory, and today my time had come. Just as Mr. Eagen turned away, darkly chuckling to himself, a fifteen-inch-long cutthroat trout, cruising not three feet from the waterline, chomped down on my unlikely spoon.

"Hey" was the only word I spoke as I brought my trophy to heel on the lawn behind me.

"What the—" was as much as Mr. Eagen could utter, for his jaw had dropped down to his collarbone.

"Well," I said, carrying the trout away (and it had such weight to it, such luscious heft), "have a nice day."

In the end that trout turned out to be something of a bum fish of singular heedlessness and gullibility, for I've never managed to catch another. But now Mr. Eagen goes into his house when I step out on my beach, and closes the drapes behind him.

Far West

I HAVE always lacked what my father-in-law calls "the bump of locality." So when I was told that Seattle was on the West Coast, I figured the Pacific would have to lie no more than a half hour's drive from my new front door. I could see, through the narrowing lenses of my Yankee spectacles, that there seemed to be a little patch of real estate between Seattle and the Pacific called the Olympic Peninsula. But it looked to be mostly national park, and I figured that like Central Park or Boston Common it wouldn't slow me up too much on a drive to the sea.

And so, not long after we got out here, Debbie and the kids and I set off one weekend for a morning's excursion to the Pacific and back. We'd seen some pictures of a place called Ruby Beach where starfish were plentiful and boulders the size of skyscrapers rose up out of the ocean. Three hours later we found ourselves still heading westward, through clear-cut forests, around mountains and lakes, past sullen backwoods towns, and it was four and a half hours before we finally sighted surf.

It was my first lesson in the scale of the Far West. Out here they are lavish with distances. I suppose as a New Englander I knew that Alaska is big, and Texas and California are sizable, but I did not know until I just figured it out that you could fit the whole of New England, all 66,608 square miles, into the single state of Washington and still have enough left over for an extra Rhode Island. In New England you may have some aspiring mountains and heaths and wet-lands and farms, but Washington is big enough to hold every variety of American landscape. It is a continental microcosm, only it's been laid out backward. The deserts, badlands, can-yons, and wheat fields of the western American landscape lie in eastern Washington, and the bustling cities and serene seaside settlements of a New England lie along Washington's western coast, with two white-capped mountain ranges for backdrop, and rain forests of almost Amazonian density thrown in for good measure.

If I were to get my wish someday and fly straight up from my front yard on Bainbridge Island, I would not have to hover much higher than my own rooftop to see not only Port Orchard Channel and the Kitsap Peninsula to the west but Hood Canal behind it and the entire Olympic range beyond. But to see the Pacific Ocean I would have to fly almost a mile farther up into the clearest sky of the year, and even then the ocean would hang from the horizon like a faint mirage.

"Are we still in Washington?" my son keeps asking on our weekend excursions east and west.

And absurdly, impossibly, I tell him, "Yes."

Home Rule

LIKE newcomers everywhere, I believe it falls to me to instruct my newfound neighbors on how to live. Consequently, I've embroiled myself in the local battle over whether or not we should stick with county government or incorporate Bainbridge Island, Washington, as a separate municipality.

For several months after I got here, I assumed we were already a municipality, and in fact when I went to Founders Day in Winslow, the island's only municipality, I thought its mayor, who appeared for the ceremony in a cheerleader's outfit, must have been my mayor as well. And in the town portrait taken there that day you may find me with my children, grinning proudly on the town's main drag.

It wasn't until a couple of weeks later that a neighbor told me that I lived beyond Winslow's city limits, and that the only local government I had to turn to was the county of Kitsap, whose seat was about a forty-mile drive away in a town called Port Orchard.

Seeing as how the island represents only about nine percent of the voters in Kitsap County, it seemed to me that if there was any sense in my regarding myself as a Bainbridge Islander, county government was neither local nor representative. And so with visions of New England town meetings dancing in my head I joined up with a group that's pushing for incorporation.

A couple of days ago, waiting for a home rule meeting to begin, I couldn't help but overhear a large, mustachioed man in a ball cap loudly ask what would happen to the parks on the island if we incorporated.

"What about the parks if you incorporate? Have you thought about that? Have you?" was how he posed it.

Well, I'd just asked more or less the same question of the Home Rule Executive Committee, so I helpfully piped up that it was my understanding that our parks would remain in a special taxing district separate from the proposed municipality.

The man slowly turned and fixed his gaze upon me. "Uh, hold it," he said. "How long have you lived on this island?"

"A couple of years," I told him, stretching things a bit.

He nodded. "And can I ask where you're from?"

"Connecticut," I said.

He nodded again. "Connecticut," he said. "Lot of history back there. Two hundred years of history."

"At least," I said.

"Well," said the man, jutting his chin, "my family's lived here for four generations, and I don't need some newcomer from Connecticut telling me about my island."

Ordinarily I'm not too bad at defending myself. Once upon a time I used to spend my car rides home fantasizing what I should have said, but lately I've stood up for myself pretty well, or, when I didn't stand up for myself, I could at least convince myself that I was probably better off remaining seated.

But this time I found I could not say anything in my defense, and merely looked away like a chastened schoolboy. The exchange haunted me not only on the ride home but the whole next day, which I spent building bookshelves in my study. Every time I measured something wrong, or bent a nail, or let a piece of molding slip under the chop saw, the longtimer in the ball cap emerged for an instant to scorn this Connecticut newcomer who calls himself an islander, who calls himself a man.

The tug-of-war between newcomer and longtimer on Bainbridge Island is probably as close to class warfare as you get out here. It wouldn't amount to anything back in New Haven, where the art of class warfare has been raised to a level of almost Oriental exquisiteness. I suspect it's a new phenomenon here, born of an influx of prosperous young couples who come here for the schools, the views, the "rural lifestyle" that the local Realtors simultaneously pitch and doom.

The island was settled and cleared of Suquamish Indians and virgin forests by lumbermen, shipbuilders, and berry farmers. A lot of their descendants are working people who are now being squeezed out by the young professionals who will pay just about anything to land on the island's beaches. So on one side you've got newcomers who fail to see themselves as part of the inundation that threatens to turn the island into another interchangeable Seattle suburb, and yet at the same time, once settled, presume to instruct longtimers on the preservation of their rural heritage. And on the other side you've got longtimers who want to be free to develop their land but resent the influx of newcomers who build their homes upon it. Thus riddled with contradictions, the two sides hurl hypocrisies back and forth at each other over issues like home rule.

I guess I resented being conscripted for this warfare, to which I object as conscientiously as possible. But the man in the ball cap had gotten under my skin for another reason. I'd been working hard at making myself at home on Bainbridge Island. I'd made friends, I'd learned the names of the checkout clerks at the market and the hardware store, I'd joined adult education workshops, I'd even thrown a neighborhood Christmas party. But what the truculent man in the ball cap was telling me was that none of this mattered. This wasn't my home. This was his home. And he was right. There are no shortcuts home, and I'm not home yet.

Scram

WHEN Jake was a small boy I read somewhere about a tribe in South America that supposedly taught its children to take charge of their subconscious by shooing away the monsters that stalked their dreams. So the next time Jake awoke crying from a bad dream I stumbled down the hall to his room and had him recount it to me, including the part where the bovine, scissor-fanged beast fed on the heads of living children buried cheek by jowl on a vast and muddy plain.

I advised Jake that the next time the beast showed up he was to tell it to scram. This was his dream, I told him, and he was the boss. *Empowerment* is what the child psychologists call it, and it seemed to work, or at least it gave Jake the courage to go back and meet the beast again.

The only trouble was that my son's monsters followed me back down the hallway and plagued the dark above my bed, like sinister exiles returned to haunt the fatherland.

Nineteen eighty-eight turned out to be one of those years that gives hope to no one but astrologers. First I had to put down my old dog Ralph, and then, as if he'd been more of a guardian at the gate than I'd given him credit for, the carport by which I buried him blew down in a storm, and suddenly my kin began to die: my wife's aunt, my godfather's wife, my wife's uncle, my brother-in-law's mother. It seemed that every phone call announced some new calamity: cancer menaced my father-in-law, and various friends and relatives suffered illnesses, setbacks, accidents, and breakdowns.

The call my wife Debbie received from our doctor one January evening was no exception. A routine mammogram had revealed a lump in Debbie's breast which appeared to be malignant. Subsequent tests confirmed his diagnosis, and for several weeks Debbie and I were entangled in a web of vital statistics. By one standard or another, the difference between Debbie's losing her hair or a piece of her breast or the whole of her breast or her life seemed to turn on a centimeter more or less of deranged tissue. So we tried to play the odds even as the odds of her survival shifted with each newly published cancer study, each expert consultation, each phone call from our distant friends.

I have Debbie's permission to report that in the end it was decided she would lose her breast, and the time came to tell our daughter, Casey. Casey had emerged from her mother's womb eight years before with a look of sympathetic comprehension that has never left her countenance. If you can have wisdom before you have knowledge, then she is wise, and no one asks Casey's opinion lightly.

So Debbie sat at the kitchen table and told Casey what was to come. At first we thought the lump was small enough to remove on its own, she told her, but now it appeared to be large enough that the safest thing to do was to remove the entire breast. Debbie told Casey that though she didn't want to lose her breast, she wanted above all else to be rid of the cancer, and if that was what it took then that was what she was going to do.

Casey listened to this and then thought for a moment, reaching forward and touching her mother's arm. "Well,

Mom," she said, "I guess half of you is going to look like me."

Only two weeks after Debbie's mastectomy she was back teaching at the University of Washington School of Nursing, and within three weeks of leaving the hospital she had regained enough use of her left arm to drag the branches of an old tree we felled to a bonfire on the beach.

Two whole years have passed without a recurrence, and with each succeeding year the chances of recurrence are supposed to diminish. But as a nurse Debbie knows that once you have breast cancer you always have breast cancer: it declares itself in the mirror, in the cautious inquiries of friends, in a hundred vagrant dreads and hesitations.

On her commutes to and from the University, Debbie is a tearer of newspapers, a circler of circulars, a clipper of coupons. At supper one evening several months after her surgery, she brought forth a flyer about a Dreyer's Ice Cream Company contest that would award a trip to Hawaii to whoever wrote the best reason why he or she should be a Dreyer's ice-cream taster. Waiting out her husband's and son's reflexive scorn, Debbie got us all to agree to give it a try, because wouldn't it be great to go test next year's flavors and win a trip to Hawaii?

As I did the dishes I realized that for the first time since her diagnosis she was ready to place a bet, however unlikely, on the future, and I thought how deeply I loved my wife and her resilience and her obstreperous vitality and goofy enthusiasms. But late that same night Debbie woke me, worrying about her prognosis. Her nodes had been clear of cancer, she'd already gone through her radiation treatments, all of the postoperative tests they'd given her seemed to indicate that they'd removed her cancer in time. But she'd just read some data from yet another institute somewhere suggesting that perhaps she should have had chemotherapy immediately after surgery, and now it was too late to do her any good.

As we talked in the dark I could see that it wasn't the study's findings that had gotten to her but the reminder that she had cancer. We talked some more and I told her what I have come to believe: that life is a matter of here and now, that whatever happened she would prevail; and in the middle of my reassurances she fell back to sleep.

In the subsequent hours I dreamed that Debbie and I were on a plane together that began to fall into the dingy evening light. I then dreamed that I awoke and grabbed Debbie, desperately hoping the crash was just a dream. But she wouldn't wake up, and, still dreaming, I began to race through the house, only to find that both Jake and Casey were gone. I realized then that Debbie and I *were* dead.

"We *must* be dead," I said aloud, "or the children would be here."

It was the first time that the fear of death had ever penetrated that deeply into any dream I could recall, although I always sense with these dreams that I've had them before. I remember other flying dreams in which my plane, manned by wide, smiling, languid men, must land on a highway, strumming power lines, pruning roadside shrubbery, ducking under overpasses. I know that the heart-thumping, parched dreams I sometimes have must bear on my mortality, but this was the first time one had followed so close behind me into consciousness.

I lay awake for what seemed like an hour, listening to Debbie's breathing. Debbie, who as mother and wife and teacher and nurse pitches such battles against the forces of darkness and inertia, was being menaced by the terror of death.

So the time had come for me to follow my own advice.

This is our life, I told the monster. *Scram.*

The Garden

SHORTLY after Debbie's breast cancer was diagnosed I resolved to build her a garden in the front yard, complete with raised beds, picket fence, and arbor.

Debbie has always kept a garden wherever we lived, even in the city. But gardening, like sewing, has me buffaloed. When we first got married Debbie tried to lure me to her side along the seed rows, coaxing snap beans and snow peas and tomatoes from the grudging soil. But finally even she had to concede that I lacked the character to put up with gardening's inexactitudes and deferments. I suppose I have pursued my own interests—writing, history, carpentry, photography—at least partially out of a fear of dying: out of a need to evade the depredations of time. I understand that gardening is supposed to make you appreciate nature's eternal cycle of regeneration, but I have never been comforted by the notion of a regeneration that will eventually depend upon my own degeneration, so I look elsewhere for the fulfillment of my dreams of permanence.

The design for Debbie's garden developed slowly on a sequence of napkins, flyleaves, and notepads. The gate, I decided, would be approached through a small, somewhat

Oriental arbor: reminiscent, I hoped, of the Japanese who once gardened on the hill behind us. And I would fashion the front corner posts out of stone to match both the new piers on the deck and the beach-rock walls of the house itself. The garden would comprise four raised beds enclosed in boxes of stacked six-by-sixes, with small bark boulevards between.

Debbie chose the spot as soon as we moved here: a twenty-by-thirty-foot plot lying along the northern boundary of our yard. The morning sun takes a while to clear the high firs by the road behind us, and to the west I had to fell a little holly tree to pierce the afternoon shade. But the garden would sit on a ledge parallel to the ebb and flow of Port Orchard Channel, and until the sun finally slipped behind the fir fringe of the Kitsap Peninsula, the four raised boxes would retain the light that beams askance across the water.

And so, like the spring spiders that had begun to survey the rhododendrons for building sites, I spent a few days traversing a web of chalk lines, plumb lines, angles, and levels, laying out the fence for Debbie's garden. I set up my table saw in the front yard and marked the dawn of three clear mornings raising its solar blade above the horizon of its milled tabletop and cutting pickets down to size.

A picket is a trickier proposition than I'd imagined; a denticulated fence can look precarious or silly or even a little sinister, like fangs, depending on its tailoring. So I consulted the old architectural manuals I inherited from my grandfather to determine its proportions. I could have been ambitious with my table saw and cut every kind of gingerbread notch and angle, but the house itself was built eighty-five years ago by island carpenters who were all business and no nonsense (and no particular skill). So I decided I was stuck with their austere and defaulted aesthetic and settled upon a simple buck-toothed version, slightly beveled at the top.

I used cedar for the pickets, and for every piece of the

fence's anatomy that touched or entered the earth I used pressure-treated lumber guaranteed by its miller to last a lifetime, and when I finished the garden and carved my wife's initials in the gate, I stepped back and admired what I had accomplished, enjoyed thinking of the fence standing there beyond my lifetime as my son's or my daughter's crops, perhaps, rose and fell and rose and fell like the neighboring channel tide.

But the next morning, when I looked down at the garden from my bedroom window, I realized that yet another of my evasions had backfired, for the garden I had built for my wife resembled nothing so much as a churchyard, with its four raised grave sites freshly dug.

A Neighborly Thing

W_E hadn't had time to feel at home out here when Debbie was diagnosed with breast cancer, but maybe you never feel at home anywhere until you meet with trouble.

Newcomers from the East feel as though they are always being tested out here in Washington, that their neighbors are poised, ready to pounce on the first assertion of eastern snobbishness. I have a penchant, or maybe it's a compulsion, to defy the prevailing custom wherever I am, and I keep flunking the test with my neighbors. I am loath to borrow sugar, I chase the neighbor's dog away, I twitch a little every time some stranger strolls across our stretch of beach. But my wife, maybe because she was born out West or because she has always been very good in school, keeps passing every test.

Our property is mushroom-shaped, with a forty-foot stem reaching down to the beach. On either side are my neighbors' houses, and since it's a climb from our house down this stem, the neighbors on the southern side get more use out of our yard than we do, and in fact take care of it and plant flowers with our blessing along its perimeter.

The Yankee in me still suspects that they must be up to something, this handsome and generous young couple with their two dogs and their truck and their motorboat. They are both lawyers, and I have caught the worst part of me wondering sometimes as they weed the flowers and water the lawn if there may be some kind of eminent domain situation developing here, if in time they might lay claim, under some obscure territorial provision of Washington land law, to this little strip of yard and eventually erect a forty-foot-wide condominium smack in the center of our view.

But then my paranoia subsides, perhaps after one of my self-conscious mentions of my claim to the little yard they tend so carefully—the only portion of our yard, incidentally, that seems to sustain grass—or maybe after they've given us, out of the blue, a plate of cookies or one of Jim's salmon that Janet has smoked.

Jim had been after me to cut down the remains of an old beachside fir tree on my property that had been repeatedly pruned and topped over the years. In the interest of community relations Debbie was all for it, but it took me a while to come around, for it seemed to me that too many trees wasn't the problem out here anymore, with so many forests toppling on the peninsula across the channel.

But in the end I decided that cutting it down was the neighborly thing to do, and would be merciful not only to the tree itself—all that was left was a truncated, dreadlocked silhouette—but to the plum trees that had been languishing in its shadow.

The second Saturday after my wife's mastectomy—one of those warm, clear, giddy days that occasionally punctuate the winter rain out here—Jim climbed up into its branches with his chain saw and felled it in sections which we then dragged out to a bonfire on the beach.

After a while Debbie joined us and began to haul branches across the lawn with her good arm, swinging her lame arm along beside her, looking not like a woman who had just lost her breast but like one of her pioneer ancestors: like the formidable Tennessee women on her mother's side of the equation who had made habitable the abstraction their husbands were carving out of the wilderness.

As the sun descended and the branches burned, first in a pale smoke and then, with a *whump,* in a roil of white flame, we sat on the seawall, drinking beer. Janet was quiet for a while, chewing on her lower lip, and then she turned to Debbie and said she had something to ask which she hoped Debbie wouldn't take wrong.

Debbie, by this time accustomed to inquiries about her operation, told her to fire away, and Janet thought for a moment more and said that she was asking this only because her mother had made her promise to.

"I told her that my neighbor was having a mastectomy," she said, "and she remembered you and she was so concerned, and then she said, 'Well, Janet. Maybe she'd like to have Grandma's prosthesis.'

"And I said, '*Mother.* How can you ask that? She's not going to want *that.*'

"And she said, 'Well, you just ask her. I mean, those things cost an arm and a leg, and it's just sitting up in the closet gathering dust.'

"And I said, '*Mother. Honestly.*'

"And she said, 'Well, Janet, it's in a *box.*' "

It turned out that not only had her late grandmother's prosthesis never been unwrapped, it fit my wife to a T.

Maybe it's a function of distance more than culture—a

friend's woes always seem worse from a distance—but when I told this story to my eastern friends, they almost uniformly shriveled up. "Oh, *no*" is how a lot of them put it.

But Debbie's reply was from the heart and pure Northwest.

"Janet," she said, giving her a hug, "this has got to be the most neighborly thing I ever heard of."

Tenting Tonight

I NEVER camped back East if I could help it, and I managed to help it until the night a few days after Jake turned five that my wife declared it was time I took him camping, as though camping had ever been a rite of passage in my house-bound family.

So Jake and I borrowed a neighbor's tent and a couple of sleeping bags and drove out of New Haven and up into the northwestern corner of Connecticut, and set up camp in an old friend's pasture. I parked the car on the road and we walked into the field about a hundred yards.

"This looks good," I told Jake, setting down the tent and sleeping bags. "You want to choose a nice, level spot," I went on, in the first burst of outdoor lore that I inexplicably mustered as the afternoon wore on: how to identify poisonous spiders, what to do if bears came by, how to build and maintain and douse a fire.

I sent Jake off to collect some dry twigs for a cooking fire, and after a trip back to the car for the cigarette lighter (for I had forgotten matches) we were soon scorching hot dogs on little forked branches and shooting the breeze.

"Dad, did you ever go camping before?" Jake asked as the sun descended.

"Oh, you bet I have," I told him. "Lots of times."

"Like—when was the last time?"

"Oh, not so long ago," I said. "Not so long ago at all."

I could see by the way Jake was regarding the deepening shadows and occasionally gripping the butt of his water pistol that these weren't idle questions. Up until about the age of ten Jake always tried hard to believe that I knew what I was doing, but I guess when the fire would only steam and smolder, and it developed that the flashlight had burned out, and the zipper didn't work on one of the sleeping bags, and my neighbor's tent had not been opened in some years and was now rank with mildew, peeling back with a sucking sound when we tried to unfold it—Jake began to take stock of his situation.

"Dad? How about if we slept in the car," he suggested brightly. "Okay, Dad? How about if we did that?"

So we tried to bed down back in the car, but at first it was too early and too light to sleep and then, of course, it was too dark and too strange, and Jake began to hear things, including a raccoon messing with my friend's garbage pail not thirty yards away: a huge, fanged bull raccoon, Jake decided, peering around with his tiny bandit eyes.

I guess the dark must have gotten to me as well, because when I tried to soothe him with a bedtime story it turned into a ghost story, and things just went from bad to worse. Complaints were lodged, advice ignored, demands made, and so about eight-thirty by the station wagon's clock we rolled up our bags and hit the road. I don't think anything we ever ate tasted so good to us as the Big Mac we consumed in Waterbury that evening, and the feature at the drive-in that night wasn't all that bad for a kung fu movie, and after taking in a Big Mac and a drive-in movie we made it home by midnight.

I think if Jake and I had lived the rest of our lives back East, we might have left it at that as far as camping was concerned.

But it didn't take Debbie long to convince me that out here in the northwest corner of the lower forty-eight there's too much to see that you can only see by camping.

And so we bought ourselves a tent and a row of sleeping bags, backpacks and fanny packs and sticks of mosquito repellent and lip balm and biodegradable shampoo, and blister tape and wool socks and flashlights and trail mix and waterproof first-aid kits: maybe five hundred dollars' worth of the simple things the simple life requires.

But I really can't complain, for in return for these investments I have camped in the pristine Olympics, and I have ridden a horse along Robertson Creek into the northern Cascades up into the Pasayten Wilderness, and fished for trout in mountain lakes. I have passed through woods lacy with wild grapevines and snowberry leaves and thistle blossoms for which the horses bobbed along the trail. I have breathed in the sharp, sugary smell of hot pine and blossoms and listened to the forest hiss of bees and gnats suspended benignly in the breeze overhead, and the mumble of trickling trailside brooks and distant, swollen headlong cataracts and streams. I have nodded off to the languid rhythm of hoofbeats on the soft forest earth that seemed stretched like a drumhead across a skeleton of roots. I have paused in a silent hollow filled with fallen trees lying like the toppled silver columns of a temple. I have passed through the dried kindling whiskers of moss on the branches of martial spears of fir along the timberline, just beyond which the trees were so stunted that we could count a hundred rings on a stump small enough for my daughter's hands to encircle. I have seen marmots creeping like fat stray cats through defiles littered with rockfalls of loose shale. I have waded among blossoms of Sitka columbine and bunchberry, Jacob's ladder, Queen's cup, snowdrops, fireweed, meadow parsley, Cascade lilies, and Indian paintbrush like sprigs of mint dipped in vermilion.

I have learned the lost art of crapping in the woods (the secret is to piss somewhere first, then find a rotting tree within an arm's length of a stand of skunkweed—or vanilla leaf, or deer-foot, or sweet-after-death: nature's brand-name toilet papers—and dig a hole in the shredded wood with a few sharp kicks of your heel). But I have not yet learned how to sleep in the out-of-doors: how to avoid that little twig under my hip, that little acorn under my knee, the rib of root beneath my left shoulder; how to put the brakes on that long, nocturnal inchworm slide to the corner of the tent; how, on a rainy night, to keep from wicking water through the sagging tent walls and the wandering corner of my sleeping bag, yea, even unto my thermal socks; how to keep from tilting all night long (forget what I told Jake ten years ago: there's no such thing in the woods as flat) and dreaming of weightless somersaults, sudden avalanches, the decks of storm-tossed ships.

But in the Pasayten I experienced a joy I have not known since my boyhood, and entertained again a boy's fantasy of a life in wild places. I wondered whether, when I got home, I would be able to put my life back together again. Or would I pick fights with my friends and scare away my family and eventually find myself back in the Pasayten, roasting songbirds and setting out punji sticks and raising marijuana?

But I seem to be all right, and at the moment Jake, for one, is glad to be under a roof again, listening to compact discs and reading books in the flat, dry, familiar comfort of his bed.

The Rescue

EVEN when the weather turns autumnal here, I remain so flabbergasted by the view from my house that on the windiest afternoons I sometimes still sit out on my deck, wrapped in an overcoat and pretending to read.

I usually have my eyes peeled for wildlife, but in the long gaps between seals and otters I content myself with boats. If a trawler isn't chugging by (one sometimes parks in front of the house all night with its blinking lights, keeping watch over its nets), then a cigarette boat is whining past Illahee, or a leisurely sloop is bending with the wind in center channel, or a restored rumrunner's cruiser putters by with its sharp and perpendicular bow and its mustachioed skipper waving from the pilothouse.

I used to figure that all these skippers were rich: the same wide, white Christian men who bustle so prosperously through the boat shows. But out here a fair number of them are what they call "boat poor," obsessives whose livings may be meager and landlocked but whose souls are exalted and always afloat. Some of the grandest boats in the sound are owned by men who live with their families in trailers, in the lofts of boathouses and the back rooms of carpentry shops: mariners reincarnated as carpet installers and Jiffy Mart operators who yearn for the days not a hundred years gone by when the harbors bristled with masts.

The boats that islanders moor offshore are tied to sunken engine blocks or truck tires they've filled with cement and studded with waterproofed two-by-fours to grip the sandy bottom. All summer long the lines hold the boats against the tide, and you can discern the channel's course by the angle of their bows as they bob off the edge of the beach.

The autumn wind along the western coast of Bainbridge Island can scud so freely over such a broad expanse of water that the channel can turn from calm to rage as capriciously as a psychopath. Consequently, most people have brought their boats in by late October, before the worst of the winter weather. There's a boat launch down the channel at Fort Ward, and last weekend a succession of my neighbors winched their boats up onto E-Z Loader trailers and brought them home for a winter's rest in their driveways.

Yesterday afternoon the air was bright and sharp, but around four o'clock the cleansing northerly breeze on the channel suddenly kicked up a froth of whitecaps. I had just bundled myself up in my deck chair like a pensioner on an end-of-season ocean cruise when I caught sight of a small green unoccupied sailboat pirouetting in the current.

I recognized the boat as one I'd seen moored a quarter-mile up my beach, and in fact I'd admired it from a distance on summer weekend afternoons as it sallied forth with its elegant maroon sails swelling with the wind. And now here it was, broken loose from its moorings and bobbing jauntily off to its doom like something out of *The Perils of Pauline.*

I am not by any means a man of action, but there was something poignant about the little boat's predicament, and, determined to set new standards of neighborliness on Crystal Springs, I told my children to watch out for me and hurried

down the hill to the water. My only vessel was a leaky secondhand fiberglass rowboat that I kept hauled up on my yard,
just beyond the tide's most ambitious reach. I had taken it
out a few times to fish and crab and drift around, but it was
a cumbersome and dowdy craft, and I always tried to row it
back to shore before the hollow place beneath the rear seat
completely filled with water, and it got too heavy to drag
back to its perch.

The tide was lapping along the little wall that separates the
yard from the beach, and I managed to get the boat out all
right and to push out into the channel. But the waves were
high enough by now to lap over the edge, and tipped the
boat so wildly that on a few pulls I missed the water entirely
with one oar or the other.

And then, after a couple more pulls, one of the screws on
the right-hand oarlock came loose. I tried to pack the oarlock
back into position and secure it by jamming a ballpoint pen
into the screw hole. But from then on I had to row gingerly
as the oarlock socket wobbled, and I wondered, pulling perpendicular to the wind, if I would miss my rendezvous with
the hapless little yawl.

Rowing a boat is a retrospective activity, for you must
always face from whence you came, and now I watched my
children on the deck of my receding house waving wanly at
their father. The hazard of drowning in Puget Sound is com-
pounded year-round by hypothermia, and I now realized, too
late, that I'd forgotten the discount-house life jacket I kept
under a plank in the yard.

And so the doubts set in. What if the oarlock came entirely
loose, or one of the gray and weather-beaten oars broke in
two, and I found myself drifting just as helplessly as the
sailboat in distress? The yawl wasn't the kind of boat that
some impoverished dreamer would own; it was more likely
an upper-class weekender's fancy, and probably fully insured.
And what if it did drift around for a while? Wouldn't the tidal

current keep it from running aground? Wouldn't the coast guard catch up to it eventually, and enter its registration number into its computer, and promptly notify its rightful owner? Wouldn't they have a harder time identifying my drowned body from the disintegrating contents of my wallet?

Just as I was feeling the extra weight of the water leaking under my rear seat—and I was finally asking myself an even better question, which was how exactly I intended to row both boats ashore when I could barely navigate the one—I finally reached the wayward yawl. Stowing my oars and grabbing my towline, I climbed into the boat and lay on its ribbed floor for a moment, rocking like a baby in a cradle. By now we were already drifting a little way past my house, and I was about to tie my rowboat to the front of the yawl when I saw that it came equipped with oars of its own: impeccably varnished oars with long shanks and wide paddles and solid oarlocks of gleaming brass.

Under the circumstances, for now seasickness was setting in, it took me a couple of extra beats to figure out that I could much more efficiently row the yawl to shore while towing my rowboat than accomplish the reverse, and so, tying my boat to the yawl's stern, I began to pull for home. The two boats were loath in the wind and chop, and at times as I rowed they hardly seemed to move at all, but we made it to shore together in a long, slow arc, and the beach stones rasped against the pristine keel as I hopped out onto solid ground.

My son helped me drag the yawl out of the receding tide and pull my waterlogged rowboat back into the yard, and the two of us headed up the beach to find the owner. Eventually, after a relay of phone calls among the wives of the neighborhood, the owner was identified, and in the gloaming, after work, he turned up in a motorboat looking dour and embarrassed.

I silently helped him push off, and he winced at the sound of his keel grinding against the stones.

"Well," he said, revving his motor, "thanks."

What did I want? A medal? A bottle of champagne? A mention in the *Bainbridge Review?* Sure. But in the meantime I figured I could get by on the adrenal thrill of my little adventure.

What they didn't tell Jake and me in the adventure books I used to read to him is that heroism, be it military or suburban, is usually its own reward. So I could see a perplexity in my son's eyes as we trudged back up to the house, for what's the difference, he seemed about to ask, between a hero and a fool?

The Enclave

NEW HAVEN, Connecticut, where I lived for thirteen years, is no model of integration. In fact, its boundaries of class and race are as well marked as any national border, and if a low-income black youth wanders over the line into some of its highfalutin neighborhoods, a customs and immigration gantlet of police is more than likely to stop him and interrogate him and send him back from whence he came.

But New Haven did at least contain a sizable black population, and I got so used to meeting black people in the street, in the stores, and on the playgrounds that their absence here in this suburb of Seattle seems to me strange and ominous and un-American: a kind of evasion, however inadvertent, of our history and our purpose.

In the three years we have lived out here my family and I have become reacquainted with a kind of suburban bigotry that I had lost track of since my adolescence in Greenwich, Connecticut, the granddaddy of American suburbs. This strain of casual racism, like botulism, thrives in a hermetic environment, and though my town has its own minorities—chiefly Americans of Japanese, Filipino, and native tribal descent—its culture is basically towheaded.

"Black kids are dangerous," one of my son's classmates declares. "My dad says that Italian kids all carry knives," a small boy announces at a writing workshop. A store clerk, deciding that I'm worthy of his confidences, informs me that the Japanese are cheap. A neighbor tells me that he "jewed 'em down to six dollars" at a church bazaar, and another neighbor declares that Native Americans are slobs.

"Go to the reservations sometime and look what they've done to their environment," he says, even as we ride in the ferry past the ravaged waterfront of West Seattle.

I'm not suggesting that there's anything unique about my community in this respect. And familiarity doesn't always breed tolerance. There's no getting around the intersection of race and class in this country, and there was a time when my son thought blacks were dangerous too, after he got mugged by a black kid from the inner-city school he attended.

But in the end Jake could name the kid who beat him up and distinguish him from the rest of his black schoolmates. It's when we separate ourselves from another people that each becomes indistinguishable from the rest. Our tolerance becomes just as fishy as our bigotry, because it's so distant and abstract, and bigotry corrodes these little enclaves into which we flee.

I don't get out much these days, but to record my commentaries for National Public Radio I must drive into Seattle every month or so and park my car near the University of Washington. The other day I was walking from the lot to the studio at KUOW when I found myself alone in a little grove of rhododendrons, and a black youth suddenly appeared at the opposite end of the glade, walking in my direction.

Back in New Haven I would have looked past the color of his skin and seen by the cut of his clothes and the purposefulness of his stride and the earnestness of his tortoiseshell glasses that he meant me no harm. But after a few years in the suburbs I could not distinguish him from the predatory youths I now catch sight of only on the tube, and I found myself ducking off the path and through the bushes and hurrying out into the world's protective view.

I stood there for a moment blinking, astonished by what I'd done, wondering what in hell the kid had made of my performance. I turned and beat my way back onto the path, but by then he was gone.

I don't know what I would have said to him if I'd caught up with him. "Sorry"? "No offense"? I've never known how to extend my apologies and convey my good intentions to black people, maybe because some of my intentions aren't all that good. I grin and nod too eagerly, I force a greeting I would never give a fellow white, and—as if black people were not really Americans but chronic foreign exchange students—I somehow try to make them feel at home.

Maybe none of us will ever feel at home in this new land, and perhaps we can't be blamed for the measures we take to make familiar this strange continent full of strange people. But if I, as a middle-class, middle-aged white man, don't feel at home here, I wonder how that black kid in the tortoiseshell glasses felt when I mistook him for my enemy and veered off our common path.

Ferry Tales

BAINBRIDGE ISLAND is connected to the Olympic Peninsula by one of those venerable, windswept bridges that make you mindful of America's infrastructure every time you cross it. But to get to Seattle, across the sound, you have to take a ferry.

The ferry boats of Puget Sound are some customers: huge lumbering slabs of steel capable of carrying over two hundred cars and thousands of people back and forth through eight miles of fog and rain and temperamental water. The *Spokane* and the *Walla Walla* service Bainbridge Island, supplemented occasionally by the *Hyak,* all of them distinguishable, according to my son, only by the quality of their video games.

Island commuters go to work at ungodly hours, some to be on hand for the six o'clock Pacific time opening of the New York Stock Exchange, I suppose, others simply because they or their bosses were raised on farms. During their early-morning crossings the ferry is a kind of compression chamber, the crossing a chance to gear up for the new corporate Seattle that the waterfront hands the ferryboat commuter on a slightly tipsy platter.

The men are pretty much in uniform by the time they embark. But a lot of women go through a metamorphosis from dowdy agrarians to sleek and frosty professionals in the zenana of the ladies' room, reportedly a jungle of hair dryers and makeup kits, raucous with gossip, foggy with hair spray.

Like most morning commuters, islanders don't cotton to much socializing. You see them raise their shoulders around their ears when they're approached, and you can pretty much tell from the angle at which they hold their papers, the minimal movement of their heads and shoulders, that they want to be left alone.

But on the way home the ferry becomes a decompression chamber, and you see women loosening their bows and men undoing their ties and whole neighborhoods gathering among the long black banquettes, where they talk about water systems, and real estate values, and the P.T.O., with occasional side trips into zoning.

Every couple of days people who drive on walk off and leave their cars belowdecks, from whence they are towed out onto the dock and impounded. People worry so much that they'll forget their cars that once in a while foot passengers will inexplicably convince themselves, just as the ferry's pulling up to the dock, that they drove on. You see them straightening suddenly in their seats, running down the aisle and grabbing their keys and darting out among the parked cars, their hands over their mouths, doubt and certainty colliding in their eyes. They'll run up one chute and down another and back up again on the other side, gulping for breath, and sometimes you'll glimpse them in the rearview mirror as you drive off, lone figures still at a loss as the last cars stream past.

Others forget as they head home that they brought their cars across that morning, and wind up leaving them parked overnight on some city street. But my wife and I have devised another dilemma. Like a lot of commuters she parks her car on the island, rides the ferry across the sound, and then takes a city bus to work, reversing the process, of course, on the way home. Some days I'll drive onto a later ferry in our other car and meet her in the city. We'll eat a meal, maybe watch a movie, and get so to talking on the voyage home that we'll drive off the ferry together in my car and ride the whole six miles home, not remembering about her car parked back at the terminal until we note its absence in the driveway. So far we've done this six times since we moved here, and never seem to tire of it.

On the face of it, commuting by ferry seems a charming way to get to work, and a lot of romantic home buyers are seduced by it on their first jaunts across the water. But ferries are prey to storms and fogs and engine failures, and there is a tyranny to the ferry schedule that is unlike even the tyranny of trains. If you miss a train there is usually some likely alternative—a bus, a taxi, a rented car. But there is no alternative to the ferry.

So there is a special anxiety about ferry commuting that gives rise to desperate behavior. Islanders will leave dinner parties before dessert, sometimes even before the entrée, just to "give ourselves time to make the boat." One man, in his frenzy, actually drove his car off the ferry deck and into the water one evening. And there is the story of the man who, late for his ferry, rushed through the ticket window and ran up the passenger ramp and flung himself across the churning chasm between the pier and the ferry, tumbling onto the deck only to discover that not only had he jumped onto the wrong boat, but it was actually arriving.

I think otherwise stable people behave this way because there is something terribly final about the sight of a missed ferry slowly pulling away. You feel sometimes as though it will never come back for you, and you will never see your island home again except as a distant gloom across the water.

This is especially so at night, when the sailings are a couple of hours apart, and almost literally so if you miss the 2:40 in the morning, which leaves you stranded on waiting room pews for four hollow hours. I wonder sometimes if this is what got the better of the derelicts who haunt the ferry terminal: once-productive island men who happened to miss the 2:40.

Prey

A DEER wandered into our lives recently, a foolish black-tailed buck mincing down our drive just as the kids and I were taking off for town. My son made me turn off the engine, and we all sat and stared at our visitor as he paused by the mailboxes with his new prongs atilt, and then passed by us on his tiptoe hooves, wobbling slightly on the driveway gravel like a girl in heels.

It occurred to us as he turned down the steep drive to our neighbor's yard that the buck was in danger, because half of the residents of our little cul-de-sac are large, loose, proprietary dogs. So we got out of our van and circled around the buck's flank, startling him in a stand of rhododendrons and chasing him, with whoops and hand claps, back up the driveway.

He skidded a little as he rounded the bend by the mailboxes, and he groaned as he found his hind footing and leapt up onto the road. Running along after him, I could feel my mouth go dry and my heart kick against my ribs, and for a moment I couldn't tell what I thought I was doing: saving the buck, taunting it, or maybe even hunting it down.

There weren't any deer back in New Haven, Connecticut. And if there were any hunters among the artists and junior professors I knew, they kept their gun cabinets and trophies out of sight. But in the Great Northwest the gun cabinet stands upright in the parlor, and the trophies stare down from the chimneypiece, and I have had to dust off my opinion.

American hunters tend to bill their avocation as a celebration of man's place in nature, but by now man's place in nature seems to me worthier of atonement than celebration. In any case, if modern life has doomed us to vicariousness, I don't see how we can reclaim our authenticity with Jeeps and guns.

But my real problem with hunting is a matter of possession. Imagine for a moment that two of us have come upon a buck in the forest. One of us is a hunter, the other an observer. During the instant we both observe the buck it is our mutual prize, or if the buck is in fact no one's prize, it is at least part of our mutual experience, standing now in a shaft of light, unaware that we're watching. The hunter raises the rifle and shoots the buck, killing it instantly before it has so much as raised its tail or snorted its alarm.

The death of that buck has not been cruel, or at least not agonizing. Certainly not as cruel as the life and death we contrive for the domestic animals we slaughter for meat, or as agonizing as what a pack of wolves or a bitter winter might have in store.

But the hunter has staked a peculiar and exclusive claim to that buck, predicated on a willingness to kill it. No counterclaim can be made by the mere observer, no matter how profound his filiation with the wild. By a hunter's logic the deer is for the killing.

The buck ran across the road and up into the woods a few yards, where he stopped and stared back at my children and me. He appeared insulted by his reception, mystified that we would not welcome such a peaceable visitor to the neighborhood.

"Beautiful, beautiful," Jake was saying as we came to a halt together, and we watched the buck withdraw into the dappled woods with his tail upraised, until all we could see was a small, receding flag of truce.

A Few Words of Wisdom
to Husbands and Wives

MARRIAGES have been biting the dust all around me lately, and it's gotten to the point where the best thing I can say about my generation is that at least it isn't burdening its children with a tough act to follow.

I've been married for almost twenty years: not very long by some standards, but maybe it's because I think of it as "only twenty years" instead of "twenty long years" or "forever" that I cling to the hope that I may remain married, perhaps even to the same person, for twenty more.

My divorced and separated friends already regard my wife and me as curiosities: doomed and simple creatures foraging in a fool's paradise. But while I don't want to be half of the next separated couple in these United States, I don't want to be half of the last married couple, either. I want company.

So I thought I would take some time off from sandbagging the house to offer up a few helpful hints for present and future husbands and wives, who I hope will accept them in the same desperate spirit in which they're given.

INDEPENDENCE

Try to get a bellyful of independence before you get married. This shouldn't take longer than a month or so. Also try to find yourself, if you can remember where you last left yourself. You'll know that you know who you are when, without anyone's help, you've developed good grooming habits and can cook a two-course meal.

IN-LAWS

It shouldn't matter who your affianced's parents are, but it seems to. Though I don't have any general rules on the subject, I've noticed that my friends haven't had much luck with ministers' daughters and stage mothers' sons.

Don't enter into little conspiracies and alliances with your in-laws, not even to arrange a surprise party. You can call your in-laws "Mom" and "Dad" all you like, but they're not your parents—they're your spouse's parents.

So try to keep your in-laws and your parents separated, even at the wedding, because one or another father-in-law is going to have a better camera or a heartier handshake, and one or the other mother-in-law is going to have a more elevated consciousness or a master's degree, and it can only lead to trouble.

SEX

Have it first, then get married. But remember that as soon as you get married it's going to change, because somewhere along the line one of you is going to realize that where you were once having a wholesome sexual relationship with somebody, all of a sudden you're sleeping with a relative.

THE WEDDING

I don't care what you believe or don't believe; don't keep the church out of your wedding, or the state, or the family, or the bum on the stoop. What you want out of a wedding is the chance to promise as many people, institutions, and deities as possible that you're going to stick together, because sticking together is the whole ball game, and you're going to need all the moral force you can muster. Promising each other with extemporaneous and conditional little speeches while waterskiing or scuba diving or standing around in shifts out in a cornfield doesn't cut the mustard, because pretty soon you'll start confusing that promise—how did it go again?—with all the other promises you're going to make and break along the way.

BEST FRIENDS

Say goodbye to your best friend at the wedding reception. Unless your best friend is married to your spouse's best friend, and they stay that way, which is not likely, your best friend and your spouse are not going to be able to stand each other, and you're going to have to make a choice. The choice should be obvious, unless of course your best friend is of the opposite sex, in which case you've married the wrong person.

FIDELITY

An open marriage is a contradiction in terms. Face it. Marriages are closed. When temptation does raise its beautiful face, try to remember that the grass only *looks* greener on the far side of the hill. Up close you'll see it's got chinch bugs and snow mold, just like home.

Better yet, have the following lines from Arnold's "Dover Beach" tattooed on your wrist for easy reference.

> *Ah, love, let us be true*
> *To one another! for the world, which seems*
> *To lie before us like a land of dreams,*
> *So various, so beautiful, so new,*

A Few Words of Wisdom to Husbands and Wives

Hath really neither joy, nor love, nor light,
Nor certitude, nor peace, nor help for pain;
And we are here as on a darkling plain
Swept with confused alarms of struggle and flight,
Where ignorant armies clash by night.

On second thought, make that both wrists.

COMMUNICATING

Speaking of confused alarms, all baby talk is out. Baby talk isn't cute, unless of course you're a baby, in which case you got married much too young.

FEELINGS

Don't ask your spouse what the matter is all the time. You aren't responsible for the way your spouse feels. You're barely responsible for the way *you* feel, so leave your spouse alone.

HELP

If your spouse is seeing a shrink, go see one too. I don't care if you're as sensible as E. B. White, as even-keeled as Perry Como—symmetry, even if it's just the illusion of symmetry, is all-important.

But remember that shrinks aren't necessarily interested in making your marriage work. They've got their own problems in that regard, so what can they do for you? Your shrink probably won't even want to meet your spouse, because that would be unprofessional or something. Shrinks, like the rest of us, don't like to face the facts, so they deny that there are any. What counts with them is what you think the facts are, even if you're crazy.

MOVING

Moving to a new place in order to run away from your marital difficulties has gotten a lot of bad press lately. But it shouldn't, because it usually works. One good place to move out of is Pleasantville, New York, but I'm sure you can think of more.

HOUSEWORK

It doesn't matter if one of you spends all day on the patio eating bonbons, you've got to divide housework right down the middle. Actual equalized work schedules, impervious to the shirker and martyr among you (shirkers and martyrs compose most married couples), should be hammered out right away and signed, preferably in blood, by both parties.

I've found, for instance, that laundry can be divided equitably if one carries it up and down the stairs and runs it through the machines, and the other folds it up and puts it away. The latter may be more time-consuming, but the former requires more impetus and brawn. When you can't divide a job down the middle, take turns doing it. Obviously none of this will work if you can't accept each other's standards of cleanliness, in which case you'd better hire somebody fast before the whole thing blows up in your face.

CHILDREN

I suppose you can sustain yourselves with cats, asparagus ferns, and social causes, but in the long run I wonder if marriage makes much sense without children. Nobody likes to make scenes in family restaurants (in fact, nobody likes family restaurants), and nobody wants little chewable plastic things on the floor, but sooner or later, after you've gotten all this other stuff worked out, you may get tired of your tidy duality.

Experts will tell you that sticking together for the sake of the children, like moving, is a bad idea. They're wrong. Children may not be enough of a reason to keep a really rotten marriage going, but they're an excellent reason to work on a marginal one, and all they ask in return is that you pick them up on time, not argue in front of them, and always let them wear what they want.

CONCLUSION

I'm afraid that's as far as I've gotten on life's highway, so that's all the help I can give you. You're going to have to handle menopause, grandparenting, and death all by yourselves. In the meantime, shape up, for God's sake, and behave yourselves.

The Whale Watch

A FEW hours after I bought the house on Bainbridge Island I watched three dolphins perform an evening recital off the side of the Seattle ferry. I don't have much patience with omens, but as the dolphins arced and dove like aquatic signatories to my terms of purchase, I figured I was off to an auspicious start in the Great Northwest, and I've been watching the water for harbingers ever since.

Our new home sits opposite the town of Illahee, which means "Home Place" in Suquamish. Illahee was the name of one of Washington State's most distinguished bordellos, but from my front porch the town seems to consist only of summer cottages, a Jiffy Mart, and a dock.

I have spent most of my idle moments on the porch of our house watching Illahee roll with the day's punches. In the morning it is a rosy apparition and at night it sparkles like a topaz necklace dropped by the shore. Sometimes it seems as though I am gazing at the reflection of my own home shore, with the light of dawn and dusk reversed.

I can't always be sure what it is I am looking for as I sit and watch the tide stir the channel like a spoon, but my ostensible ambition is to sight a whale. It has always been a long shot, for whales are usually sensible enough not to duck across from the Pacific through the Strait of Juan de Fuca and lose themselves in the bewildering polluted maze of Puget Sound.

Along the mile of water that stretches between Illahee and me I have seen seals, bald eagles, blue herons, kingfishers, skunk ducks, and cormorants, and huge lumbering beasts I am told may be surfacing sturgeon. I didn't buy the sturgeon scenario until a hundred-year-old, six-hundred-and-fifty-pound, eleven-foot-long expired sturgeon floated to the surface of Seattle's Lake Washington recently, thereby verifying the outlandish reports from fishermen and water skiers of a lake monster that devoured ducks, surfacing occasionally like a waterlogged sequoia before sinking back to the bottom.

One evening this summer I was dislodged from my watch post to take the family and a couple of house guests out to dinner. As we drove along Crystal Springs Road, my daughter recognized a buddy of hers named Erin fishing with her grandfather from the old public dock. We waved and proceeded by, and I remember thinking how nice it was for Erin to fish with her grandfather, even if they weren't likely to catch anything but bullfish among the pilings.

It wasn't until the next morning that I heard about the whale. It must have approached our house just as I rose from my rocking chair, and it must have passed by as we climbed into the van. It passed Erin and her grandfather only a couple of minutes after we drove by, a lone mature gray whale sounding and breaching fifty yards off the tip of the dock.

Like the jealous suitor of an unfaithful lover I grilled Erin about her sighting. Could she hear it spout? Could she see its bovine, cue-ball eyes? Was it as big as a ship? A house? A school bus? Was it big enough, I wanted to ask her, to send its wake splashing up against the pilings and singing its praises on the gravel beach? Big enough to lure the gulls to the shallows along its back? Big enough to find its way home to the ocean?

"I don't know, Mr. Ward," Erin told me. "It was big, that's all I know."

So now I have climbed back into the crow's nest of my front porch, my eyes peeled for the ocean's most extravagant possibility, a lone beast heaving past my house like a ship, or a school bus, or a colossal, preposterous dream.

Eggs

ALONG the shoreline below our house only one empty building lot remains, a grassy rectangle squeezed between the houses of the Fieldses and the Brooms. I suppose we should enjoy the lot's vacancy while it lasts, which can't be for very long, but instead my neighbors and I worry it like a scab. The lot engenders a pained expectancy. *Leave it alone or do your worst,* we want to tell its owner, because the suspense is killing us.

Jim Fields owns a truck, a boat, an RV, and a collection of antique cars that threaten to gridlock his garage and driveway, so he has inquired to see if the owner might sell the lot to him in order to expand his own premises a little. But the lot seems to be tied up in the settlement of its late owner's estate, and in any case his widow is in no hurry to let it go.

A couple of days ago Jim called me over to show me something he'd come upon while he was out on the lot, cutting the grass.

"I almost hit 'em with the mower," he said, pointing down at the ground.

At first I couldn't tell what he was talking about, but then I finally registered a humble congregation of small, buff eggs lying out in the open by a tuft of grass.

"It's my guess they're killdeer eggs," Jim said, pointing out toward the water, "by the way that one over there is carrying on."

Out on the beach a small brown and white bird was making a pitiable spectacle of itself, shrieking its own name and limping around across the pebbles with one striped wing outstretched.

The killdeer is a small banded plover the size of a large sandpiper and just as trim and nimble a dancer when it hunts for food along the lapping beach. But it has a distinguishing knack for diversion and feigns injury whenever intruders approach its nest. If its predators are swift enough the diversion may well cost the killdeer its life, but usually it makes itself just conspicuous enough to lure its enemies away from the shallow declivity of its nest before flitting off over the water, miraculously recovered.

Jim and I backed away from the eggs and marveled awhile at the killdeer's ploy, at the millennia of evolutionary increments it must have taken to perfect its deceptions. But it pains me a little to startle a bird, because of the energy they expend and thus must recover whenever they take to the air. So I wish the killdeer would save itself the trouble.

But a killdeer can't distinguish between predators and those of us who live on the beach and take our constitutionals along the channel's edge, and so they play their protective scam for us, screeching and limping, whenever we venture near. Maybe it's a distinction a killdeer can't afford to make, for however much we may believe in our own benignity, our residence here is costing most of the wildlife on Puget Sound its habitat, and even those of us who treasure these nervous little neighbors of ours do more damage to the killdeer's prospects than any marauding fox or raccoon. We are not so easily distracted from our purposes by the killdeer's charade, and our depredations set like concrete.

I have brought my son down to look at the eggs once, but otherwise we've all tried to leave them alone, hoping they will hatch and their occupants will survive to enact their own parental flimflam when their turn comes. And so they remain on the open ground, and some nights I think about them out there, expressions of pure geometry in a chaos of grass, camouflaged only by the speckles on their pale shells, protected only by their mother's chicanery and man's occasional mercies.

Oil and Water

I GOT home on New Year's Day after a holiday jaunt back East to learn that a couple of days before Christmas a barge had been rammed by its tugboat off Grays Harbor on the central coast of Washington and had leaked 231,000 gallons of oil into the tide.

The scale of the catastrophe crept up on people out here. At first they had no idea so much oil had been dumped, and then they thought the stuff would flow southwestward, away from the pristine beaches and sanctuaries of the Olympic National Park. But over the weekend the wind kicked up and drove the goo northward.

By the time I got to the bird rescue center that had been set up in a convention hall in the beachside town of Ocean Shores, people were finding contaminated birds washed up along the mouth of Puget Sound, and globules of oil were lapping the coast of Vancouver Island.

A normal oil spill, and we live in a time when there *is* such a thing as a normal oil spill, may claim 300 to 400 birds. But this spill killed about 4,000 scoters, grebes, murres, loons, canvasbacks, old-squaws, auklets, puffins: the bobbing birds of the Pacific surf who gather in these waters for the winter. As of the Friday after I arrived, 6,610 birds had been brought in, 3,851 of them dead. Of the remaining 2,759 live birds, 800 had either died from shock or languished so miserably that they had to be killed.

The majority of the survivors were murres. In the wild the murre is a vigorous fisher-bird, as regal and comical in its elegance as a penguin, which it resembles, with a black back and wings and a buxom, snowy breast. But you wouldn't have known it to look at the murres people were catching on the beaches and bringing to the center in bags and nets and cardboard boxes. You would have thought they were naturally torpid and the color of railroad ties.

The same went for the grebes: fierce and frail with their flat-top crests and blood-red eyes and long necks and beaks. And for the scoters: as livid-billed and querulous as Daffy Duck. And even, finally, for the few shy loons that survived long enough to reach the center, where their pens were shaded and hushed over with sheets.

Some of the birds were so contaminated that they had to wear bibs to keep from ingesting oil when they groomed themselves, and so in bibs they padded forlornly over beds of newspaper and rag in the jerry-rigged plywood pens that covered the convention center's half-acre of floor. The Ocean Shores Convention Center may never smell the same again after a residence of a thousand defecating fish-eating birds.

Park service rangers, National Fish and Wildlife functionaries, and state environmental officials ran the operation at the center, but it was staffed almost entirely by volunteers: students, retirees, birders, bikers, homemakers. Few of them had ever handled live birds before. They were given rubber gloves and garbage bags to wear over their clothes. The birds had a tendency to empty out when you lifted them, but the gear was really more for the birds' protection, to keep us from contaminating them further with the oil on our hands and clothes.

Volunteers did everything from crumpling newspaper for bedding to tube feeding the birds three times a day with a protein gruel. The main order of business was getting the birds cleaned so they could replenish the natural oil in their feathers and return to the wild. But the wild was still too compromised, and some of the two dozen washed and banded birds that were released before New Year's washed up on the beach again, soaked in oil. Eight hundred and fifty birds had been cleaned by the time I left, but no more were to be released until the oil finally dissipated, and so they huddled and preened in net-bottomed pens.

The people who came here to minister to them became engaged in an anguished communion. The birds were not grateful to our species for their circumstance, and did not welcome our ministrations. They quite naturally assumed that each time we scooped them up we were going to eat them, and so they did their best to slash and snatch at us with their strong, sharp beaks. But it was no small thing to hold a wild seabird, and people who cleaned the birds seemed to become imprinted on them. Just as they exulted when the bathed birds were finally released in the holding tanks outside, they sobbed and grieved when a murre died of shock in their arms.

In the fluorescence of the hall the volunteers roamed the narrow paths among the pens, moving slowly, shushing each other like librarians as they passed the loons. But even though the volunteers were driven by altruism, they had to keep it in check in order to sustain the most likely candidates for survival.

I learned this lesson circulating through the hall, feeding smelt to the grebes and murres and scoters. The temptation was to try to coax the lamest birds to eat and to shoo the most persistent birds away. I saw more than one kindly novice standing by a pen murmuring and waving a solitary fish at some poor, hunched nicknamed stray.

But in fact, you had to pelt the birds a little to get their attention, and flip the smelt when you tossed it so it registered as a fish before it landed in the camouflage of newspaper and rags. And you had to toss a good many fish at once so the murres wouldn't waste their declining energy on shuddering, twisting tugs of war.

You had to be a little less aggressive with the grebes, or they would think they were under attack and sound a shrieking alarm. Both the grebes and the murres, when given a chance, daintily lifted the raw, thawed fish from the floor and tossed it until they could swallow it headfirst in a couple of outstanding gulps.

The scoters, being ducks, were always falling out among themselves, and did each other injury with their gabbling bills. They made almost as quick work of a smelt as their neighbors, but they chomped at the fish sideways, devouring it in stages. Though their bills are blunter than the grebes' and murres', the scoters were more valiant, and snatched at your legs if you tried to approach them.

All the birds looked pretty miserable at first glance, the murres gathered forty to a pen. But these birds comprised a kind of aristocracy of the fittest. They'd already survived an ordeal of contamination, hypothermia, starvation, dehydration, capture, shock, injection, handling, and imprisonment. The cadavers of their weaker cousins lay tagged and frozen in a locker, to be used as evidence in the event of a suit.

But even these hardiest birds were languishing. You can tell if a bird is dehydrated by the protrusion of its keel, and if it's anemic the inside of its beak turns bright orange. Some of the sickest birds lay apart from the huddled groups with their oily wings outstretched. You noticed them blinking their eyes more slowly, or holding their beaks open as if gulping for air. Some grasped feebly at the fish that was offered and then shook their heads, as if politely declining. They bunched together in the corners of the pens: some of them, I think, to keep warm, or maybe they had just followed the plane of a plywood wall, trying to escape.

There's probably no underestimating the intelligence of these birds, but it didn't do to patronize them. Their simplicity is surely more benign than the stupidity, say, of an oil company or a tugboat captain or the rest of our heedless species. Some suspect it may not have been the initial spill that contaminated the birds that eventually washed up as far north and east as Port Angeles but the discharge from other boats and barges that seized this opportunity to dump their waste into the water.

Before driving home I walked past the retaining tanks, where a pair of burly loons were paddling after their baths, and I headed out toward the beach for a stroll.

There were a few gulls and crows huddled high up the dunes and a couple of sanderlings trotted back and forth with the tide, but nowhere in or beyond the surf that rose almost a half-mile offshore could I spot a single bird, or hear a single call on the cold ocean wind.

I have always found beach walks restorative, but it seems that oil spills taint not only the ocean but our perception of it, so that even its natural sheen and luminescence becomes suspect. It is hard to imagine that any number of gallons of oil man can carry and count, even up into six digits, can compromise such a vast expanse of surf and sand. And yet I found myself second-guessing the reflection of the gunmetal clouds and peering suspiciously at the brown sand churning in the surf.

Spa Defender

THE most serious people I know are in the leisure industries, and the uniformed baritones who came to install the hot tub were no exceptions.

But hold it—there I go again.

"This is not a hot tub, Andy," the senior installer informed me the last time I slipped up. "Hot tubs are primarily of wood construction. This unit is fiberglass, Andy, and so it's called a spa."

Spa, hot tub, whatever—the thing now hums discreetly in my side yard, out of sight of the casual visitor to our door, a bubbling hexagonal stew of hose water and Leisure Time spa additives: chlorine, baking soda, polymer scum-collecting agents, and something called Spa Defender, a liquid bulwark against calcium buildups.

The hot tub represents a first-round knockout punch my wife delivered in the spa-versus-boat dispute that began shortly after we received, out of the wild blue yonder, a refund check from the IRS. That the money, technically speaking, had been ours all along never seemed to occur to either of us until it was too late. It seemed more like a gratuity, like play money, out of reach of necessity, philanthropy, or good common sense.

I traded punches with Debbie for the first minute of the

first round, but when I had to admit that I was miserably prone to seasickness in small boats, Debbie saw her opening and struck. By the time my head had cleared, the hot tub was rolling down the driveway in a trailer.

So I helped the spa crew heave the damn thing into position, and as the installer filled me in on pH levels, test strips, four-function air-generation systems, and all the rest of it, my attention wandered, and as I always do when my attention wanders, I tried to make a crack.

"Boy," I said, "I had no idea leisure was so much work."

"Andy," sighed the installer, whose name I didn't catch, "your spa has been designed to provide years of pleasure and satisfaction with a minimum of effort. And the sooner you learn how to read its needs, Andy, the sooner you'll experience that pleasure and satisfaction."

I know he's right, of course, because every now and then I fail to read a need, and something aberrant happens, like buying a spa. On chilly nights when my family is out parboiling itself under a splash of stars, I have tried to imagine that we were Swedes perhaps, or maybe Finns, and that lolling around in hot water was somehow good for our characters, like a kind of Lutheran austerity.

You're supposed to be careful in spas. A couple of glasses of white zinfandel and you can percolate to death. But as I emerge pale and steaming, like a soggy dumpling from a tepid stew, and as my watery footprints follow me upstairs, I'm afraid of drowning not in the spa's hydrotherapeutic jets but in bed, asleep, in a thick and sybaritic soup.

Parents Night

DEBBIE and I are about to celebrate our twentieth wedding anniversary, but it wasn't until Parents Night a little while ago that I realized what odds we've been bucking all these years.

Like most parents, we don't ask a lot of our children, only that they live up to our potential. From kindergarten through graduate school Debbie was a straight A student. And so in our scholastic lectures to our children we try to dwell on Debbie's example, since my own academic career probably would have ended, and definitely should have ended, about midway through high school, but for a kindly man named Nomer who gave me a D instead of the F I so richly deserved in chemistry. In fact, if not for Nomer, I might still be in high school, grizzled and flatulent in the back row, pounding my brow to make it think.

So for me, Parents Night at the high school is a nightmare. I dread the fluorescence of the cinder-block hallways; the totalitarian whiffs of disinfectant; the bulletins, buzzers, and bells; the pallor of the principal's jowls as he now addresses us, the parents of grade nine.

I am suffering all this again for my son's sake, amen, I tell myself as I crowd with the other parents into the assembly room. But I am choking, I am going blind, and in my ringing ears the principal's greeting is all slip-slapped and contrary. I fold and twist my son's schedule until it's indecipherable, and I can't for the life of me figure out what I did with the high school hallway map.

But not to worry, for Debbie is here, my wife of twenty years, my dear son's mother. She stands now on tiptoe amid the others, craning toward the principal, leading the laughter at his little jokes, nodding at his homilies, and making certain, as she applauds him, not to crumple the pristine schedule and map she carries neatly under one arm.

I slog after her from class to class, and as I sulk in the rear of each room, glowering at my son's teacher while she recites her semester's worth of goals and expectations, Debbie sits far forward at her little front row desk, assists the teacher with her handouts (making certain I get one too), and raises her hand eagerly to ask questions.

Where did I find this little brownnose, anyway? I ask myself, fiddling with the jackknife in my pocket. And where did she find me, a forty-three-year-old man who wonders now if he were to sneak his knife out of his pocket and carve something into the top of the desk whether the kid who usually occupies it would get the blame.

Just so long as it isn't me, he tells himself as the warning bell sounds, and Debbie gathers her handouts into a tidy little pile.

And you know what I'd carve if I still had it in me, if I could get away with it, if I only had the guts? I would carve my wife's initials, and mine beside hers, and enclose it in a valentine. Isn't love the damnedest thing?

Fruitcake

*B*ACK when Debbie and I were newly married some friends of ours took to sending us an annual holiday fruitcake. Sometimes they'd bring it over, sometimes they'd send it, although the shipping nearly killed them. The thing was the size and shape of a small snow tire, and studded not only with fruit and nuts but—and here was what really set it apart— marshmallows.

We always made a fuss over it in front of our friends, but we called it Perpetual Fruitcake around the house, and it used to lie around the house for months. It got so that when the next fruitcake rolled around, most of the last one would still be moldering in the rear of the refrigerator. So we would heave the old one out and heave the new one in, and there it would sit for the rest of the year, a dark and brooding presence somewhere behind the cheese.

In the little town where we lived every church sent out carolers. I enjoy singing Christmas carols and will brook no groans on the subject of Christmas in general, but one year it got out of hand. The local Episcopalian minister challenged the other churches to see which congregation could raise the most joyful noise, and for the four or five evenings preceding

Christmas the doorbell would ring, and we would go down in our shirtsleeves and stand with our arms crossed at the threshold as successive throngs of Baptists, Episcopalians, Catholics and Congregationalists, Presbyterians and Methodists, and a huddle of breakaway fundamentalists who worshiped down the street in the Boudins' garage, stood out in the snow, raising a song as dense and wavering and temporary as the steam that rose from their mouths.

Sometimes we would join in with them, but usually we just stood there, nodding and grinning and conducting with one upraised finger. We always tried to have enough cookies around to pass out before the carolers proceeded down the street, but one evening the competition got so fierce that some of the ensembles began to double back and sing at us again after other groups from other churches had moved on, and no sooner had we called out our thanks and handed over our cookies to the Methodists than the Episcopalian choir, led by the hearty young minister who'd started the whole thing in the first place, appeared at the top of the driveway, singing at the top of their voices.

By now something in us had turned against these herds of Yuletide trick-or-treaters, and as the Episcopalians reached their final plagal cadence I think the same thing occurred to Debbie and me at the same time.

So Debbie fetched the fruitcake, and we distributed chunks of it to everyone. You could see their mittens sink a little under the weight of each slice, but they beamed at us in the dim porch light and set forth for the next house, shouting their thanks over their bundled shoulders.

"No, no," we called out. "Thank *you*."

Word must have traveled fast about the treat at the Ward house, for only one more throng came by that night, and the next morning, as if cows had been herded through, the snowy street was littered with little clods of cake.

The Essaymatic 5000

I LIKE to think of myself as someone to whom time doesn't mean very much. It's not that I've come to grips with my own mortality or found solace in the infinite; it's just that I work at home and take my cues from my wife's and children's arrivals and departures, the cats' scratching at the door, the clank of the mailbox when the mailman slams it shut.

But sometimes, when I've invited the Taplins for dinner at six or promised my brother that I'll call back at nine, I have to know what time it is. Since my wristwatch spends most of the day on the rim of my bathroom sink and is in any case of the limited-warranty drugstore variety, my most reliable source for the time of day is the telephone.

After a few spins of the dial I can reach, at any hour of the day or night, the recorded voice of a person I imagine to be a sprightly, gray-haired lady—now, dead, I've somehow decided—cheerfully ticking off the remaining hours and minutes of my life. Her eternal recitation has the eerie quality of an all-night diner, but it's a service of the phone company and gets the job done.

What bothers me are the little prefaces the Time Lady delivers before she gets around to the time. "An energy-saving tip from the phone center store—form car pools and combine trips" is her message at this moment (10:12), but I have heard her take swipes at letter writing, hawk push-button phones, and remind me of faraway loved ones I haven't called in weeks (although she displays a curious lack of concern for the loved ones I haven't called who live within my toll-free area).

She is a fund of advice and information, but she has a somewhat scolding, Dr. Joyce Brothers lilt in her voice and I always hang up with a mortified feeling. In fact, sometimes I get so snagged on her pitches and tips, so inspired to close my fireplace dampers or call my Aunt Ruth, that I forget to hear what time it is and have to start the process all over again.

I hate to sound ungrateful, but since the Time Lady is paid out of the profits the phone company makes by overcharging for its other services, I tend to regard her as part of Ma Bell's product line, and as such she demonstrates to me once again the increasingly preachy and grudging manner in which business has taken to dispensing its goods and services. Promotion, which was once an antecedent to actual commerce, now survives each transaction and sticks to each product like fly-paper. In fact, I've lately gotten the feeling when I buy something that I've merely entered into a sort of joint ownership arrangement with its manufacturer and that what I like to think of as my possessions will always have their hearts back at the factory, like campers longing for home.

I've always resented the little logos that mar my appliances: "F/GM/Mark of Excellence/Frigidaire/Product of General Motors U.S.A./Imperial 170" on my refrigerator, "Sears Kenmore Magicord Powermate" on my vacuum cleaner. It sometimes seems to me, as I look around the honky-tonk of my kitchen, that I've spent my money only to populate my shelves and countertops with ambassadors singing their companies' praises. Even now, as my typewriter taps out these words for me, it is advertising SCM's Smith-Corona Coronet Super 12, while in a far corner of the house my radio blows its horn for Sony.

Certain kinds of products have mysteriously escaped the chrome nameplate and the Technicolor decal. Furniture, for instance, still functions purely as furniture, ungarnished by promotion. But I don't think it will be long before we'll see convertible sofas with "Castro" stitched into the upholstery or rugs with "Karastan" worked into the weave. Clothes were once off-limits in this regard, but now people seem to get a warm, participatory glow from wearing Adidas T-shirts, Yves St. Laurent ties, or designer jeans with "Calvin Klein" emblazoned across their backsides.

Even the post office has begun to put its dowdy wares to promotional use. A few years ago my godfather, a Dante scholar, rushed through a purchase of fifteen-cent stamps only to discover later that they were a new variety no doubt devised to counter the Time Lady's attacks on written correspondence. Each of them was decorated with a floral generality and a motto: "Letters preserve memories," "Letters lift spirits," or "P.S. Write soon." The purchase thus transformed my octogenarian godfather, of all people, into an involuntary press agent for the Postal Service. My godfather insisted in one letter that the stamps were the work of the Hallmark people. "Who else," he wrote, "but one—or a committee—of their hired poets could have conceived such sentiments?

"And I can't afford to burn them," he added in an apologetic footnote. "One of them is affixed to this envelope."

Nor have the states been left behind. For a time New York was considering putting "I Love New York," on its license plates. E. B. White saw this coming, along with everything else, some decades ago, when Maine stamped "America's Vacationland" on its plates. But I think New York would have gone Maine one better. I don't believe states should be allowed to put anything on their plates other than the necessary letters, dates, and digits, but if that isn't possible, and it doesn't seem to be, New York ought at least to make the plates adjustable so you could change "I Love New York" to "I Like New York Okay" or "I Don't Mind New York" or "I Don't Like New York Very Much," depending on how you feel. Otherwise, they confuse the meaning of "I"—something I'd like to keep straight as I trip along life's highway. I'm all for states' rights, I guess, but I don't think states have the right to enforce our affection for them.

I once walked into my baby daughter's room to get her up from her nap and found her standing in her crib and flashing me a strangely flawed and gaping smile. Upon investigating further I discovered that she had chewed the logo tag off one of her stuffed animals and was in the process of swallowing it. I hooked it out of her mouth with my finger, and after I calmed down a little I tried to explain to her that though the label was a good one, for we've tried to buy her nothing but the best, it was not worth dying for. But she gave me a patronizing look and slowly shook her head, and I knew that Casey, like her brother before her, would someday don Sea World sweatshirts and refer to life's necessities by their brand names.

Her father, however, hasn't given up the battle yet. You might think that I just like to bring this stuff up and not do anything about it. Well, then you've got me wrong, for I think I've finally found a cure for our sickly pride of ownership.

It turns out that many of these logos I've been complaining about are removable. The plastic SCM/Smith-Corona Coronet Super 12 logo plate, for instance, came off without a hitch, and after a little light scrubbing with a sponge you'd hardly know anything had been there. And all it took was a few quick turns of a screwdriver and the Sears Craftsman logo came right off my mower. I haven't had quite as much luck with the GE/General Electric decal on the front door of my toaster oven, but I'm working on it. The only real problem I've had is with the logo plate on the refrigerator door. I pried it off easily enough, but it left a long scab of glue which now gives the refrigerator a sullen look.

Removing the logo plates has given most of my possessions a pleasing, abstract quality, but I think what I'll have to do in cases like my refrigerator door is devise logo plates of my own to paste over the scars the old ones leave behind. I figure I could find somebody who could fashion a few for me out of brass or chrome, and in the meantime I think I've figured out what they should say. I think if I'm going to set a good example for industry I'd better keep my own name out of it, but I'll have it read in simple little letters: "A poor thing, but mine own."

Clear-cut

I SUPPOSE that most of what I take for wild forest out here
in Washington is an illusion, no more than perhaps a hundred
years' worth of second growth. By the turn of the century
the virgin coastal forests of Puget Sound were gone, and the
view from Port Orchard Channel was bald as an egg when
my house was built in 1905: bald enough at least to reveal a
vast view of the Olympics that has since been reduced to a
few distant crystal shards sinking behind a rising evergreen
tide of second growth.

But beyond the crest of the ridge that lies across the water
from my house, the last acres of America's virgin rain forests
are toppling. In my Yankee ignorance I used to equate national forests with national parks, and figured that the vast
green zones labeled national forest on my northwestern maps
were sacrosanct. I now find that they aren't protected so much
as managed, and that last year five and a half billion board
feet of wood was lumbered from national forests in Washington and Oregon alone. That's more than twice the amount
lumbered in 1982, and would have beat 1987's record but
for an inconvenient spate of forest fires.

So I seem to have moved out here in time to witness the
last of the mortal wounds we've inflicted on the wild, to drive
through mile after square mile of clear-cut stubble, of torn

and splintered roots and stumps. History buffered me from such prospects in New England, whose virgin forests fell over two centuries ago. There was even some rueful solace to be had in the reassertions nature now makes upon an eastern landscape compromised by Western man for over three hundred years. But in Washington the virgin forests are still falling, and it struck me as I drove through the clear-cut ruins of the Olympic Peninsula's forests that where the search for nature in the East might lead you to a shaded, ivied graveyard, out West it takes you to battlefields still smoldering, still littered with the dying and the dead.

America, America

THERE'S been so much fuss made lately about burning the American flag that I wonder why no one's paid any attention to the terrible thing each and every one of us is guilty of doing to our national anthem: namely, singing it.

I've heard it a thousand times at ball games, town meetings, school assemblies, and TV station sign-offs, but I never knew anyone who could sing "The Star-Spangled Banner" without defacing it, and I wonder if Congress, once it's done fire-proofing the flag, would consider legislating that only those with trained voices and a comfortable range of, say, three octaves be allowed actually to perform our national anthem, while the rest of us just stand there moving our lips.

But "The Star-Spangled Banner" must be an awfully undemocratic anthem for a democratic state if only a tiny aristocracy of vocalists can even sing it. And maybe it's so hard to sing because it's such a turkey to begin with. Francis Scott Key may have had every right to his siege mentality back when the foreign devils were upon us in the rockets' red glare, but this country hasn't really been directly under siege since the War of 1812, unless you count the times we've laid siege to ourselves.

"The Star-Spangled Banner" seems an awfully generic and truculent jingle for a nation as great as this one. "Our flag was still there"? Well, you could sing the same thing about the flag of Albania, it seems to me, assuming that it's spangled. All countries have flags, and somewhere along the line, even with all those "bombs bursting in air," their flags kept standing too.

So what I propose is that we fold up "The Star-Spangled Banner," with all due ceremony, and pack it away in a time capsule, maybe, or the Smithsonian Institution. What we need is an anthem that talks about something more than the durability of dry goods and the dangers of fire and dares at least to make a passing reference to our ideals and aspirations.

I thought "This Land Is Your Land" was the best bet for a replacement until I heard Ray Charles at the 1984 Republican National Convention. Now Mr. Charles can turn even "My Bonnie Lies Over the Ocean" into something transcendent, but it took a great song to give me the patriotic thrill I experienced watching a convention that had just nominated Ronald Reagan for a second term, and that song was "America the Beautiful."

Here's an anthem—written, incidentally, by a teacher named Katharine Lee Bates—that, so long as we stick to the first verse, is short and simple enough for a fullback to sing, and praises not only this uniquely various landscape we occupy, but our stubborn hope of getting along with one another. In fact, it tells us that if we intend to stay on this beautiful continent we'd better be worthy of its splendors.

O beautiful for spacious skies,
For amber waves of grain,
For purple mountain majesties above the fruited plain!
America! America!

And here comes not a boast but a plea.

God shed his grace on thee
And crown thy good with brotherhood
From sea to shining sea!

Thank you. You may be seated.

Bill

A SINGULAR hazard of life on Bainbridge Island is marine mammal dung. Otter droppings dot the boats at Port Madison, and seals occasionally relieve themselves upon the Winslow docks. But in our neighborhood it was old Bill, the lone bull sea lion, who befouled my neighbor's swimming float, and every few low tides or so I'd catch Mr. Grady marching with a bristle brush out across the beach to sweep Bill's mementos under the waves.

Bill made a regular spectacle of himself this winter. I had a hard time believing my eyes the first time I spotted him sleeping in the sun on the Gradys' float. At first glance Bill was just a burlap hump of something, like a sodden sack of sand. But then I'd sight a flipper, or make so much noise crunching over the barnacled stones that he would wake and grunt and turn his head around to face me, and meeting his, my eyes finally had to admit that this blubberous mound was indeed a living thing.

And then Bill would dive, and the float, liberated from the oppression of his bulk, would bob jubilantly above him as he slunk among the waves awhile, waiting for me to pass. Sometimes I would hide among the exposed roots of the Whitmans' beachside cedar and peek around its trunk to catch sight of Bill poking his mustachioed, Prussian head up out of the water, checking to see if the coast was clear. And then with an impossible lunge he would flop back up and sit sleek and vigilant on the teetering float, belching and sneezing and yawning, expectorating salt water and scratching his chin with his tail.

But sometime around late March Bill stopped coming to call. The worry was that he'd ventured over to the Ballard locks across the sound and gotten himself nabbed in a sea lion trap—part of the valiant effort by an amalgamation of state, federal, and tribal fish and wildlife people to restore the population of steelhead, a variety of sea-run rainbow trout that used to spawn in such abundance in the rivers that empty out into Puget Sound. Steelhead grow to as much as forty pounds and are prized by fishermen not only for their sweet and silky flesh but for hitting hooks like locomotives.

When the Ballard locks were built in the early 1900s to make the sound accessible from Seattle's Lake Union, they cut off one of the steelhead's chief spawning routes, and now even with the introduction of a ladder the great iridescent fish balk and stall in the churning spill from Lake Union's gates.

It did not take long for word to spread among the sound's burgeoning sea lion population that the locks offered a superlative dining experience, a kind of twenty-four-hour all-you-can eat special, and great numbers of them gathered to feast languidly on the crowds of steelhead lagging in the foam. It's been estimated that a single sea lion will consume anywhere from fifty to three hundred pounds of steelhead a day.

Except for a few stray orcas that sometimes venture down from the San Juan Islands, the sea lion has no natural predators in these waters, and since it is now a protected species it can't be shot. So the state has been reduced to trying to shoo these adroit beasts away. They tried nets, they tried horns, they tried firecrackers, but after ten days or so it all seemed only to garnish the feast, like a floor show.

In the end it was decided to trap the sea lions in cages and ship them two hundred and eighty miles out to the ocean. But they underestimated these sea lions' devotion to their favorite eatery. Of the thirty-seven sea lions trapped and shipped off to the ocean, twenty-seven came back from their seaside vacations, asking for menus.

The solution seems to be to cover the pristine bottom of the locks with enough debris to provide the steelhead with hiding places, but the proposition is entangled in the network of agencies contending with the problem. In the meantime people continue to call in with a lot of advice. One suggestion is to float a model of a killer whale in the vicinity, but evidently this has been tried in California, and after a few days the sea lions got so used to it that they took to sleeping on it overnight. Others have suggested importing a shark, a live killer whale, and even an "attack polar bear," though none seem to be currently listed in the Seattle Yellow Pages.

Fishermen, of course, are not amused. The sea lions at the Ballard locks ate sixty-four percent of the already-precarious population of steelhead last year. Only five or ten years ago sport fishermen could go out for a couple of hours and guarantee themselves a steelhead or two, but nowadays they can troll and bob and cast spoons all day and come home with nothing to show for their troubles but a mildewed slicker and a buzz on. So it's no excuse but no wonder that occasionally a frustrated fisherman will pick up a rifle and forget the federal law against killing the sea lions who occasionally swim by with prize steelhead flopping from their jaws.

It was hard to tell if that's what happened to Bill, for the dead sea lion that washed up on the beach a couple of weeks ago was so battered and bloated that they couldn't find a bullet hole. Indeed, they couldn't even figure for sure if it was Bill or some other of his brethren. It's true that he hasn't shown himself in the last couple of months, but then he always did stray off to northern ports of call during the summer. So we won't mourn until autumn. In the meantime everybody misses Bill, even Mr. Grady.

The Bedtime Story

*F*OR parents and their children bedtime is supposed to be an enchanted interlude of solace and confidences and lullabies. But nothing can break the spell for some parents like the request from a child for a bedtime story.

Some people are born storytellers. Listening to them weave their tales, you'd think they'd spent their whole lives in a rocking chair, whittling sticks and spinning yarns. They seem to have made some mysterious connection with the universal subconscious, and from their mouths—complete with sound effects, songs, and accents foreign—a personal folklore burbles forth like water from a spring.

You might think that my children were privileged in this department to have a writer for a dad, to have a novelist at their bedsides every evening delving deep into his fertile imagination and weaving magical extemporaneous tales worthy of direct transposition and eventual paperback sales. But as Jake and Casey will tell you (or won't tell you if they want dessert), I am a miserable storyteller: an Aesop with writer's block, a constipated Uncle Remus.

If their request alone didn't panic me, the words "Once upon a time" would, and before I knew it I would have dragged Jake and Casey into some murky and ill-governed kingdom full of characters with such spur-of-the-moment identities as Fletcher Fly or Connie Condominium, with no plot or moral or resolution in sight: an unraveling universe of caprice and random disaster.

If my children fell asleep, I was saved. But more often than not they stayed awake and alert, expectation losing to doubt in their large, intelligent eyes. I would get Grover Groundhog wishing for some reason that he were a chili bean or Phil O. Dendron lamely longing to be picked, and then, finding no other exit, I would turn to, say, Jake, and ask, trying to mask my desperation, "And what do *you* think happened?"

"I don't know. You're telling the story."

"I know that. But I thought you might like to guess."

"No."

"Why not?"

"I don't want to guess."

"Well then," I would say, rising to my feet and tucking in his blankets, "you think about it tonight and I'll tell you what happened at breakfast."

It was one of those ploys for which parents justly hate themselves: right up there with "Grow up" and "We'll see" and "Act your age." Perhaps you have never stooped so low in the storytelling business, but before you do, I thought I ought to take a stab at devising some tips for bedtime yarn spinners. Even if I turned over a new leaf by eight o'clock tonight it would be too late for Jake and Casey, who have now taken to telling *me* bedtime stories, but there may yet be hope for you.

THE BEGINNING

Never begin a story with the words "Once upon a time," not to mention "Once, in a kingdom far away." These will only remind you of the story you blew the night before, or of the great classics of the past to which your story won't be able to hold a candle.

Don't start until you have the beginning of a story in mind. This should be self-evident, but it isn't, because a lot of people expect the story to tell itself. It won't.

DELIVERY

Anyone who's tried to tell one of Jack Benny's jokes will confirm that delivery is everything in storytelling.

This isn't much comfort if your timing is lousy, but it's cause for hope if you're working with shaky material, which you are. (Besides, I'm offering advice here, not comfort, so try to pay attention.)

If you reach the point where your voice begins to double back on you like diet cola aftertaste, your only hope is to turn the story over to somebody else. All of us carry alternate personalities around with us, and the best way to reach them is by speaking in their voices. Even if you've got a tin ear you must be able to affect at least a couple of different accents. I have had some luck with Lyndon Johnson's and Alistair Cooke's. I don't know why—maybe we all carry around with us some other person waiting in the wings for a schizophrenic cue—but an accent helps a story take on a life of its own. Of course, you may run the risk of getting stuck and scaring your children to death, but do they want you to tell them a bedtime story or not?

SOURCES

Just because you're making up the story doesn't mean you've got to do it entirely on your own. All great artists steal stuff, and so should you. People think the only appropriate source for fairy tales is Old World folklore, preferably of the Black Forest variety, which sticks them with witches and trolls and transcendental frogs and a lot of other things we don't know anything about. Give up this paralyzing prejudice and start putting your own folklore to use: comic books, *I Love Lucy* episodes, office gossip, class action suits, soap opera scenarios. We've all got this stuff taking up valuable storage space; we might as well put it to use occasionally.

CHARACTERS

Most children's stories are about children and bears and elephants because it's easier to make up stories about children and bears and elephants. Don't discard such species just for originality's sake. If you're going to start casting aardvarks and bustard quails for your story, be sure you know something about them. Of course, if you've already blurted something out about, say, anemones, and you don't know anything about anemones, then forget their anemoneness: dress them in pantsuits and put them someplace familiar, like a housing development.

THE SCENE

Always set your stories in countries ruled by monarchs. Tyrants tend to clear the air, and—let's face it—symbolize parents. Besides, your characters need to be able to find a policeman when they need one.

PLOT

Everyone can make up a plot, or in any case adapt one. The trick is to know when you have enough of a plot to get the job done. Overplotting is the storyteller's downfall, so keep it simple. All Barry the Bear has to do is go out into the snow—when all the other bears are sleeping—and get cold and hungry and afraid and wind up going back to bed, and you've got yourself a plot. He doesn't need to have a philosophical debate with Crandall Crane or fall in love with

Beatrice Beaver or follow Old Fogey into the Slaw of Cole. You don't have all night.

THE END

Be sure you can tie up all the loose ends of your story when the time comes. Tidy conclusions are what your children are looking for, and who can blame them when the room is dark and there's a scratching at the window?

If you've got to come up with a moral, try not to be too pushy about it. The old Naughty-Ned-gets-his-comeuppance scenario went out with birching and detachable collars. In storytelling as in life, preaching won't get you into heaven, and since it serves no other useful purpose you might as well drop it entirely.

Find it in your heart to let the child triumph in the end, if only by sheer force of will. Kids need to feel powerful as they enter their dreams, and besides, you can always throw your weight around again in the morning.

Well, I don't know about you, but I feel a whole lot better. I recommend your putting these suggestions to work this very night. Just because they haven't worked for me is no reason they shouldn't work for you.

So good night, sleep tight, and don't let the bedbugs bite.

Fantasia

W*HEN* Jake was three years old some friends of mine played a recording of *Peter and the Wolf,* and as he listened we all hovered over him, translating each peep of flute, each indignant bluster of bassoon. Jake stared back at us as if we had all gone crazy. It wasn't the story that bewildered him: he and I had been reading a Disney Golden Book of *Peter and the Wolf* that he had selected off a motel gift shop magazine rack the summer before. What worried him instead, I think, was the obstructive notion that music, which up to that point he had accepted on its own terms, had to represent something in order to mean anything at all.

Almost from the time Jake was born he loved to listen to music. The only way I could get him through his infant bouts with colic was to press him against my stomach and carry him around the yard, singing "We Are Climbing Jacob's Ladder" in a rumbling baritone. And as soon as he was able to get to his feet he began dancing to music, gravely rocking his head back and forth like a baby elephant lost in thought. What he heard didn't conjure up Russian forests or regiments of wooden soldiers or bestiaries. What he heard instead in the records I played was a beautiful, moody, organized noise.

What I heard, and maybe what Jake eventually heard as well, was Tubby the Tuba sobbing in the park, Mickey Mouse

drowning in a forest of brooms, hippos dancing, lovers part-
ing, surf, Mexicans, cannon fire, and 1930s traffic, sometimes
all at once. And for that I blame all those composers and
music teachers, entertainers and cartoonists who believed
that the only way to interest children in music was to illustrate
it for them.

My fifth-grade music teacher, a narrow detrimental named
Mrs. Pramm, believed this with all her heart. She had us close
our eyes and envision things with her as we listened to dam-
aged library records of classical works.

"And now the little fawn is getting to its feet," she'd say
in her jolly singsong, "and listening for his mother, who's
coming—do you hear the French horn?—coming around a
boulder—do you hear the boulder?" And when the works of
great composers refused to conform to her little scenarios,
she punished them with jingles: "This is the symphony that
Schu-hoo-hoo-bert never fi-hi-nished" or "It's number one!
It's number one! It's number one by you-know-who!"

I sometimes wonder if some notable composers studied
under Mrs. Pramm or one of her ancestors. I see Grofé
handing her his *Grand Canyon Suite* wrapped around an apple,
Copland raising his hand in the front row, Respighi receiving
an entire box of gold stars for piping actual birdsongs into
the *Pines of the Janiculum.*

To this day I will catch myself closing my eyes to Bach or
Mozart and seeing geese tricycle through the woodwinds,
starlings pizzicato from the treetops, satyrs fall upon what
sounds to me like the trumpeting ranks of the League of
Women Voters. And some days Beethoven or Brahms will
plunge me into such a confusion of images that I have to rush
out of my chair, turn off the stereo, and listen for a while to
the unmetamorphosed silence.

Miranda Mouse

*I*F Seattle conjures up any architectural landmark in your imagination, it is apt to be the Space Needle, an insectile tower that rises out of Seattle Center, a congregation of buildings left over from the 1962 World's Fair. Up to now Seattle Center has been a benign if decrepit complex of restaurants and fairground rides, an arena and an opera house, a mall and a couple of museums, all linked to downtown by a monorail.

As part of an overall effort to jazz up Seattle, the city fathers have asked the Disney people to come up with a master plan to turn the center into something more exciting. Now, for better or for worse, Disney people bear about as much relation to their late founder as, say, Con Ed people bear to Thomas Alva Edison, but I still think this may be as good a time as any to trot out a story my friend once told me about a trip she took to Disneyland. I present it as a cautionary note before the city fathers innocently skip into the neo-Bavarian order of the world according to Disney.

One winter my friend Alice decided to visit her brother in Los Angeles. Just before departing she received a letter from an old high school friend she hadn't seen in over a decade. The friend had somehow gotten wind of Alice's visit and proposed that the two of them spend a morning together at Disneyland, catching up on old times. So on the appointed day Alice drove to Disneyland and found her friend standing with her husband by the ticket booths. Alice didn't recognize her at first. In high school her friend had been something of a hellion, but now she was dressed primly, and when she smiled at Alice she seemed thinner of lip and wider of eye than Alice remembered.

During the course of introducing her husband, Alice's friend announced that the two of them had recently found Jesus, and during the hours that followed she thanked her Lord more than once for the glorious time they were all having. In fact, she didn't have much interest at all in catching up on old times. She seemed to dismiss old times as a period in her life when she was floundering in the darkness of unbelief. What she wanted to talk about now was Alice's future, and whether there might be any room in it for her Savior.

Thus the afternoon proceeded in Walt Disney's Wonderful World of Waiting, until finally, as the three of them cued up for the Matterhorn ride, Alice's friend glanced down the line and caught sight of a shaggy young man furtively puffing on a joint.

"Well," declared the friend, "this just spoils the whole family feeling. I'm reporting that young man to the authorities."

And with that she stomped off around a corner.

"That's my girl," her husband said a little sheepishly. But before Alice could reply, her friend was rounding the corner again and pointing out the fellow with the joint.

"*That's* the man," she said, crossing her arms and rejoining Alice, who swears to me that the three of them then watched as Mickey Mouse and Donald Duck padded up to the young man, grabbed his arms in their three-fingered mitts, and dragged him off to never-never land.

I like to end this story by having them read him his rights in piping falsettos, but I'm afraid I made that part of it up.

Yumbo

WHEN my niece Kelly Susan was ten years old, I sat down to dine with her at an inn. She was handed the children's menu, a little folio of selections printed on construction paper in gay pastels. It gave her a choice of a Ferdinand Burger, a Freddie the Fish Stick, or a Porky Pig Sandwich.

Like most children's menus, it first anthropomorphized the ingredients and then killed them off. As Kelly read it her eyes grew large, and in them I could see gentle Ferdinand being led away to the stockyard, Freddie gasping at the end of a hook, Porky stuttering his entreaties as the ax descended. At that time Kelly Susan, alone among all her family, was a resolute vegetarian and had faced up to the dread that whispers to us when we slice our steaks. She wound up ordering a cheese sandwich, but the children's menu had ruined her appetite, and she spent the meal picking at her food.

Restaurants have always treated children badly. When I was small, my family used to travel a lot, and waitresses were forever calling me "Butch" and pinching my cheeks and making me wear paper bibs with slogans on them. Restaurants still treat children badly; the difference is that lately restaurants have taken to treating us all as if we were children. We are obliged to order an Egg McMuffin when we want break-fast, a Fishamajig when we want a fish sandwich, a Fribble when we want a milkshake, a Whopper when we want a hamburger with all the fixings. Some of these names serve a certain purpose. By calling a milkshake a Fribble, for instance, the management need make no promise that it contains milk, nor even that it was shaken.

But the primary purpose is to convert an essentially bleak industry, mass-marketed fast foods, into something festive. The burger used to be a culinary last resort; now resorts are being built around it. The patrons in the commercials for burger franchises are all bug-eyed and goofy, be they crane operators, grandmothers, or priests, and behave as if it were their patriotic duty as well as their God-given right to con-sume waxy buns, translucent patties, chewy fries, and industrial-strength Coca-Cola.

But happily the patrons who actually slump into these places are an entirely different matter. I remember with fond ad-miration a tidy little man at a Burger King in New Haven whom I overheard order a ham and cheese sandwich.

"A wha'?" the girl at the counter asked, fingers posed over her register.

"I wish to order a ham and cheese sandwich," the man repeated.

"I'm sorry, sir," the girl said, squinting down at her key-board, "but we don't carry ham and cheese. All we got is what's on the board up there."

"Yes, I know," the man politely persisted, "but I believe it is up there. See? The ham and cheese?"

The girl gaped at the menu board behind her. "Oh," she finally exclaimed. "You mean a *Yumbo*. You want a *Yumbo*."

"The ham and cheese. Yes."

"It's called a *Yumbo,* sir," the girl said. "Now, do you want a Yumbo or not?"

The man stiffened. "Yes, thank you," he said through his teeth. "The *ham* and *cheese.*"

"Look," the girl shouted, "I've got to have an order here. You're holding up the line. You want a *Yumbo,* don't you? You want a *Yumbo!*"

But the tidy man was not going to say it, and thus were they locked for a few moments, until at last he stood very straight, put on his hat, and departed intact.

Here and Now

*T*HERE are only about a thousand acres of farmland left on Bainbridge Island, including berry patches and gap-toothed stands of Christmas trees, and the consensus seems to be that in a couple of years it will all be gone. Nevertheless, the first thing people talk up on Bainbridge Island is its rural atmosphere.

I think for a lot of us that's really all we mean: atmosphere. After all, most of us have only a storybook acquaintance with farming, and sustain our agricultural heritage by doing maybe a little gardening, catching a couple of commercials for breakfast cereals, and occasionally stopping in the country at a roadside stand.

Bainbridge Island is famous for its wine-dark and honey-sweet strawberries. In fact, they became such a favorite of the voluptuaries of the Tenderloin that ships used to sail in from San Francisco just to load up on them. Our raspberries are just as fine, and to this day a produce sign announcing Bainbridge Island berries draws eager customers in Seattle's Pike Market.

But farming was never exactly a gold mine on Bainbridge Island. The Japanese who constituted most of the berry growers out here started farming berries and Christmas trees by default when the Port Blakely Mill began to lay off its work-

ers, and the Filipinos and Canadian Indians who moved here
took over for their Japanese employers when the Japanese
were incarcerated during World War II. Those who returned
and stayed on are now elderly, and for some of them farming
has become vestigial and avocational.

These days farming seems to have fallen into the crack
between the proponents of the take-the-money-and-run dy-
namic of development and those who believe that the only
benefit people should derive from the earth is spiritual or at
least aesthetic. What most of us mean by rural is really just
open space, and if the measures by which we seek to preserve
open space—strictly residential zoning, for instance—eventually make it impossible for farmers and their descendants
to stay on the island, then that's a trade-off the rest of us are
willing to make. Few of us have much tolerance for the flip
side of farming anyway: the manure and the stoop labor, the
runoffs and the pickup trucks and the rusted-out tractors in
the yard.

So I keep wondering if, once the last throes of the island's
agronomy are over, the best we can hope for is the kind of
"rural atmosphere" I encountered as a teenager in the back
country of the zoning-pioneer community of Greenwich,
Connecticut, where an exalted uniformity of means has land-
scaped the dappled roads with restored barns (festooned with
agricultural implements but containing guest rooms, studios,
fleets of antique cars), remodeled farmhouses, lawn tractors,
Arabian horses, and artfully grouped stands of daffodil among
the great pruned oaks.

I can get just as misty-eyed as the next man when I drive by
fields of corn, but I think we Americans are all mixed up
about our agricultural heritage—in fact, about our heritage
in general.

When I was visiting Greenwich a few months ago, I stopped

and ordered lunch at Friendly's, and because it was a Friendly's, and not a Quickly's, I had a lot of time to think. The restaurant was decorated in a converted-barn motif with mock beams made of wood-stained Styrofoam and Masonite wainscoting lined with Colonial-style coat hooks. Hung here and there like hunting trophies were bits of rusted agricultural flotsam: gate hinges, horseshoes, a cast-iron tractor seat, a pitchfork with a busted tine. Even my Formica banquette had a weathered look beneath its polished surface, like barn siding coated in ice, and between the doors to the rest rooms and the dishwashing pit were several balsa wood collages suggesting covered bridges, farmhouses, and fences.

It seemed to me a shame to see all these mementos of our rural past lending their authenticity to a proposition as antithetical as Friendly's. It reminded me of all those "You're doin' great, America!" ad campaigns that play on our nostalgia to sell such futuristic wares as diet cola and airline tickets. What a corruption of our nation's folkways, I told myself. What a perversion of our most cherished notions about family, community, and country.

But before I could really get myself worked up, I caught sight of a boy I'd known slightly in high school. He was in his forties now, like me, and sat dressed in a three-piece suit, dabbing at his mouth with a napkin. Despite his suit and a certain pallor to his jowls he looked very much as I remembered him: tidy, close-cropped, and serious.

"You poor son of a bitch," I heard myself mutter as he solemnly tucked into his little paper cuplet of coleslaw. "You never got away."

I surprised myself with my own vehemence, but where my musings about the preciousness of our rural heritage had been intellectual, my scorn for my old schoolmate had come straight from the gut. So I had to ask myself why. If I really did cherish my heritage so much, if I really did care about roots—why was I so contemptuous of my classmate's decision to stay put? And if I thought there was something wrong with him for having stayed in his hometown, did I really mean all that stuff about America's sweet and simple past?

Maybe I was wrong to be so hard on my old classmate just because his and my paths of least resistance had led in different directions. There are hometowns, and there are hometowns, and maybe I wouldn't have felt the same way if my schoolmate and I had grown up in some little town in Iowa.

But I began to suspect that Friendly's decor and my own protective romance with the past were really of a piece. Friendly's thought all these agrarian accessories would give its franchises a cozy feeling and take our minds off the assembly-line cuisine of which we are all supposed to be so deeply ashamed. But the sparse rustic trappings on the mock-weathered walls instead gave the whole enterprise a halfhearted feeling, as if Friendly's itself would have preferred to exist in the days before there was electricity and refrigeration and all the other technologies that make Friendly's possible.

It seems to me that every time we try to soothe our troubled selves by evoking an edited and pacified past we wind up making ourselves feel all that much worse for living in the here and now. *You think this food is something?* we tell ourselves like nostomaniacal old codgers. *You should have had Grandma's cooking. You like this town? You should have lived back when a town was a town and neighbors knew their neighbors. You think you've got a family? You should have seen the families they had a hundred years ago: everyone pitching in, fathers working side by side with their strong-backed sons, all the daughters helpful and virginal, all the children loving and beloved and respectful of their elders.*

I am no historian, but I've done enough required and avocational reading of history to agree with Lord Macaulay that no one "who is correctly informed as to the past will be disposed to take a morose or desponding view of the present." From what I've read, the American past would be a nice place to visit only if you weren't poor or Indian or black or Jewish or Hispanic or female, and then only if you got all your shots, packed your own lunch, and brought your own drinking water.

I think we may envy our forebears for running their courses, for laying to rest in their own graves the doubts that plague the living. But what we really long for is not the past, which was at least as hazardous and brutal and heedless as the present, but another chance at our own lives. Our nostalgia has a wistfully authoritarian streak because the old-time security we hanker after is the security of childhood, when somebody larger, older, and wiser interceded on our behalf.

This yearning for the good old days takes a lot of wind out of our sails as it puffs up the windbag of political rhetoric, with its glorious legacies and shining futures. What gets left out is the present, or, to put it another way, what gets left out is reality. The present exists solely as a litany of problems to be addressed in the past's name and for the future's sake.

We deprecate the present because it doesn't lend itself as readily to abstraction. People are too well acquainted with the present to be fooled about it very much, so it's no wonder that politicians prefer to appeal to the foggy, dreamy images of the past that even the most ravaged of us nurture and to our starved and excitable fantasies and fears. For politicians the unedited continuum of the present is indigestible.

Thus, we long for the past because it had such confidence in the future even though that future is now the present from which we long to escape back into the past—are you following this?—while we dream of a future predicated on the very ideals of the past that have brought us to this supposedly unhappy present.

But compared to the known past and the uncertain future, the present doesn't seem all that bad. For my part, for instance, I didn't even exist for most of the past, and I am not betting on existing for most of the future.

"No more deadly harm can be done to young minds," said

Alfred North Whitehead, "than by the depreciation of the present. The present contains all that there is. It is holy ground; for it is the past and it is the future." I think I agree with this, although I'd prefer it if Al had kept the past and the future out of it (along with that semicolon). The chronicles of Camelot and the blueprints for Utopia are fictions, and we ought to take at least a little pride in being facts.

Maybe that's why I prefer to eat at diners along the highway that serve meals in the same stainless-steel surroundings in which the food itself is unabashedly prepared: eateries free of the kind of homey touches that can only remind me that I am not at home.

So what I'd like to tell Friendly's and remind myself is that authenticity derives not from nostalgia but from the courage of our own time and place. The intelligentsia of his time regarded him as a dinosaur, but Winston Churchill had that courage when he defied the Nazis and the Bolsheviks and all the other self-styled champions of the future. And it seems to me that what should concern us more than nostalgia or fantasy is the people with whom we share the present. The time is now to face the facts, because the facts, by God, are us.

The Eagle Watch

I FIND more and more that I don't like to leave Bainbridge Island very often. It worries me, now that I think about it, but no destination seems to me worth leaving home to get to.

It worries my wife even more, and she's always trying to shake me loose. Thanks to her, the wall around our kitchen calendar is a collage of concert broadsides, park district schedules, invitations, contest forms, alerts, and announcements. She awakens with a start each morning, animated by agendas, and her first words to me are usually logistical.

"Wake up the kids," she told me last Sunday dawn, darting out of bed, "and tell them to dress warmly."

I rolled onto my side. "Dress warmly?"

"For the eagle watch."

"The what?" I mumbled, squinting out the window into the cold and drizzling dark.

"The eagle watch on the Skagit River," she replied from the bathroom. "I told you about it weeks ago. Weren't you listening? Don't you remember?"

No, I guess I hadn't been listening, and now all I remembered about eagles was standing out in the driveway one fall afternoon and feeling a compression of air about my shoulders and ducking around to see a bald eagle flapping its great wings not twenty feet overhead. Its talons dangled beneath it like an old man's knuckles as it followed my driveway up to the street, and one yellow eye glared back down at me from its white, indignant head.

All I ask of a Sunday is a day of rest—no strings attached, no bells or buzzers or maps or instructions: a dreamy blur of dropping in and dropping out and dropping off to sleep. But now I had to rouse my sleeping children and coax them into long johns so that we could accompany Debbie out to Battle Point Park at the crack of a gray and gusting dawn and pile into one of the park district's vans to look for somebody else's eagles.

Three hours later the sleet had turned to snow along the serpentine banks of the Skagit River and clung to the mournful, sagging little hemlocks and the moss on the cottonwoods that overarched the road. Here and there in the distance we saw a little clot of shadow, like a cocoon on a twig, and the park district guide would hit the brakes and roll down his window and point into the snow.

"There's one," he'd say. "But gosh, I wish he was a little closer, don't you?"

We stopped at a Nature Conservancy lookout where the eagles were even more disdainful and remote. The rain kept blotching our binoculars, and I was afraid I was going to short out my video camera, which I'd brought along with notions of acquiring footage worthy of the *Nature* series.

A hearty fellow from the Conservancy, all beard and boots and L. Bean machismo, arrived with a busload of birders and visitors and gave a little talk on the habits of the distant eagles, that now appeared, even in our binoculars, like tiny specks of ink.

"Someone has asked me if bald eagles are playful," he called out at one point. "Yes," he said, "bald eagles are playful."

We all ate our lunches and drove around bleakly for several hours, peering into the cottonwoods. All told we counted thirty-nine eagles, but we never did see one up close. And it seemed wrong to see so many eagles at once. Their majesty is in their solitude, and yet here they had gathered like so many chickens: henhouse biddies peering down at the drift boats floating by.

Neither I nor my children ever complained to Debbie. No, we never complained once. Not once. But my videotape came out looking kind of grainy, and when I show it to friends— and what lucky friends I have—I must go up to the screen and point out the hunched and backlit shapes of eagles bobbing among the pixels.

The weather cleared the next morning, and as I was walking the beach my neighbor came out to greet me.

"Boy," he said. "You should have been around yesterday afternoon."

For it seems that not twenty feet off his deck a bald eagle had attacked one of the American wigeons that take up winter residence off our beach. It was amazing, my neighbor said, how stubborn that eagle was, for the wigeon kept diving out of reach, and it took the eagle ten minutes of diving and rising and circling and diving before it wore the wigeon out so badly that the poor duck couldn't fold its wings and the eagle finally snatched up its quacking prey and carried it off in a trail of feathers.

"I tried to phone you," my neighbor said, "but I guess you weren't home."

Exactly.

We Must Not Do
This Again

MAYBE your dinner guests are all delightful, and as far as you're concerned they can never overstay their welcome. But I've got a couple of people I know from long ago with whom I am caught in a now-we-owe-them-dinner cycle that we can't seem to break.

As far as I'm concerned, there is no such thing as a brief visit with these people, and as the evening enters its middle years I grow more silent and sullen. They, however, do not, because nature abhors a vacuum, and naturally enough, the less time I use up talking to them the more time they have to talk to me.

It's not their fault that we don't have anything to say to each other, any more than it's my fault that we don't have anything to say to each other. But the most important thing I think we all have to keep in mind is that we don't have anything to say to each other.

I would not countenance the embarrassment and hurt feelings I am no doubt risking by bringing this up if I didn't think the rest of you might benefit somehow from my experience. But I finally figured out who's responsible for this eternal social cycle we're caught up in.

It's me.

And do you know why? It's because of something that

comes over me when the evening finally draws to a close. I get happy. I get expansive. As soon as—let's call them Rick and Marge—as soon as Rick and Marge start heading for the door, I feel such relief, such profound and exhilarating joy, that do you know what I do? I ask them back. I ask them *back*. And in fact, the more dreadful the evening the happier I am to see it end, and thus the more insistent I become, as I help them into their coats, that we really must do this again, and soon.

I don't know if there's much I can do about it, because in this brief and woeful life it seems a terrible thing to contain one's joy. But maybe the trick is to bring the evening to a close *before* the joy kicks in: abruptly and firmly and finally to a close.

So now I'm rehearsing a line I've learned from Robert Watkinson Huntington, my wife's late paternal grandfather, an accommodating but nonetheless self-respecting Yankee of the blue-blooded variety who I think deserves a special citation.

When his own Rick and Marge lingered too long in his parlor, he would slap both his knees, rise to his feet, and declare to his wife, "Well, Connie, let's go to bed and let these nice people go home."

A Classic Confrontation

I *HAVE* just spent the week with my wife's family in California, and have come home once more with a chastised feeling. My father-in-law is a man whose intellectual range encompasses everything from the juvenilia of Jane Austen to the closed-versus-open universe controversy, and who, of an afternoon, reads Pascal in French.

My own intellectual scope is such that I initially misspelled "Austen" with an *i* (and besides, have her dimly confused with Charlotte—or maybe Emily—Brontë, whom I haven't read either). And I have to put Pascal with such other imponderables as Spinoza and (excuse me while I reach for my Bartlett's) Aeschylus, Trollope, Racine, both Plinys, and a host of others at whose mention I knowingly nod and desperately try to change the subject.

I've been lying about the great works of Western literature for years. I used to get by on the *Classics Illustrated* comics and the plot outlines with which I sometimes faked my book reports, but that was a long time ago. *Masterpiece Theatre* has helped a little, but they haven't serialized *Tristram Shandy* yet, or anything by Boswell, Marlowe, or Pope. Of course, nothing short of actually reading these fellows is going to solve my problem, but nothing is more dispiriting than trying to read something I've claimed all along to have read already. Besides, I have the reading speed of a congregation reciting from an updated prayer book, and a decision to polish off, say, Plutarch's *Lives* is as great a commitment as painting the house, or driving to Nebraska, or having another child.

Still, I am always so ashamed by my father-in-law's insatiable literacy that every time I visit him I try, at least for a while, to read his frayed, beloved copy of *War and Peace.* In no time, however, I am sitting unnaturally straight by the window and thinking, "Here I am at last, actually reading *War and Peace,*" and losing my place among all those sons of 'viches. Perhaps if I were left alone, I might actually follow through. But someone is always coming along and casually remarking that he or she likes to return to *War and Peace* as to a well; or wonders how someone my age, with my interest in literature and history, could possibly have waited so long; or tells me that I am reading the wrong translation; or claims that *War and Peace* is, after all, vastly overrated, and that if I really want to read Tolstoy at his best, I should read *The Death of Ivan Ilyich.*

Someone once accused John Lennon of lifting one of his lyrics from Proust. (I think it was Proust, but I can't be sure it was Proust.) Lennon countered that he had never read any Proust, and that since he had arrived at the lyric on his own, he must be as original and ingenious a thinker as Proust was. I enjoyed his reply for a while, until I realized that Lennon, like me, probably had no way of knowing whether he had ever read a little Proust somewhere, or maybe some secondhand Proust in another man's writing. I am always devising little epigrams, only to be told that they have already been articulated, and discredited, in one form or another by a whole string of fellows in nineteenth-century Germany.

"Here," my father-in-law says, bringing a volume of Schopenhauer off the shelf. "I think you might find this enlightening."

So I put down my copy of *The Making of "Jaws"* and forlornly pick my way through Schopenhauer. "A man who has no mental needs," he tells me, "because his intellect is of the narrow and normal amount, is, in the strict sense of the word, what is called a philistine."

Wait a minute, I tell myself, turning the book around again and glaring at its spine. *Who was this chucklehead anyway?*

Alarms

I_T used to be that you could smoke anywhere you pleased
on a Washington State ferry, or anywhere you damn well
pleased, as a lot of longtimers put it. Then the Surgeon General's report came out and smokers were banished to two
areas amidships. But car passengers had to pass through these
sections to get to the smoke-free areas, and there were a lot
of complaints from nonsmokers, or "newcomers," as a lot of
longtimers call them.

So now smokers have been banished to the top deck and
to areas at either end of the ferry, which are open to the
wind, and it would not surprise anybody if eventually the last
of the Northwest's smokers wound up being towed across
the sound in dinghies, bobbing in the ferry's wake, puffing
in the rain.

I suppose there may be such a thing as a right to smoke,
but it doesn't compare to the right to breathe, which is having
enough trouble these days without people blowing smoke in
its face. But however idiotic smoking may be, a lot of longtimers see the establishment of nonsmoking areas as part of
a larger phenomenon, another alien encroachment on the
right to be left the hell alone that was the reason people's
ancestors moved all the way out here in the first place. I guess
I share their aversion to anyone telling me what's good for

me, or even what's good for them, and I can sense, I think, that by means of such strictures, however reasonable and beneficial, the Northwest is bound to lose some of its spirit: its ranginess.

People talk about the rise in crime out here, and pine for the days when you could leave your car and house unlocked, when you used to feel secure. But the old days here were probably more capricious and hazardous than today, so I'm beginning to think that what they are really hankering after isn't safety so much as a time when people were still willing to take risks. Peril was one of the primary spices in the north-westerner's stew, along with solitude and self-reliance and the mystery of untrammeled places. But with each new wholesome stricture, with the tide of development and the decimation of the forests, the recipe shrinks and the flavor fades.

I was asked for my ID by one of the newest businesses on Bainbridge Island last week—the first time anyone on the island has asked for my ID in the two years I've lived here. In fact, I was asked for two IDs: a driver's license and a major credit card. I suppose the credit card was just supposed to corroborate my license (though what the credit card really provides is a separate kind of proof: that I am bonded by debt to my fellow Americans).

But it made me mad, and I still can't kick my lingering indignation and the gnawing sense of culpability I feel whenever I'm suspected of something I not only didn't do but wouldn't do, at least not yet. In fact, I think that I am now a little more capable of doing whatever it is they're afraid I might do because they have suspected me of doing it in the first place.

When somebody challenges my identity they pull the rug out from under my feet. Maybe I'm not who I am, I begin to postulate. Maybe I don't live where I reside, and I am just a Gypsy passing through.

In any case, the trust I'd had in the store when I entered into our transaction was broken, and now I readily reciprocate its gratuitous suspicion, for whenever I go back I always give them the third degree on the freshness of their wares, and I pay with plastic and take a special pleasure in tearing my carbons in front of the clerk and carrying them out the door.

But like suspicion itself, which has a tendency to stain, the carbons smudge my hands, and I am brought full circle. Tearing carbons is as much a newcomer's trait out here as requiring two forms of ID, as characteristic of the new actuarial order as asking for letters of reference, as paving the driveway, as installing outdoor lighting to pierce the brooding dark and then, blinded by the glare of our paranoia, setting off our own alarms.

Boat Sick

I BOUGHT myself a boat today, a ten-year-old fifteen-foot Boston Whaler with a seventy-horsepower Evinrude, complete with trailer and related attachments. Discounting the leaky little rowboat that came with the house, I have never owned a boat before. In Greenwich, Connecticut, where I misspent my adolescence, boating was so compromised by the imperatives of yacht clubs and sailing derbies that it seemed to offer all the romance and adventure of a round of golf.

But as soon as I moved out here people began to tell me that I had to have a boat. *Live on the water in the Northwest without a boat?* I had to be kidding. So I began to travel the boat show circuit, casing the market for a craft that might serve my purposes, and hoping, in the process, to figure out exactly what those purposes might be.

I've lived on a channel, which is to say beside a channel, for three years now, and every day I've spent a few minutes watching the speedboats and sailboats zip and meander by. I suspected that there was a whole other geography out there of straight lines between points, or ports, or public docks, free of cars and roads and bridges. I supposed that if I ventured out across to the opposite shore from my house, I might look back to find that all this time Mount Rainier has been watching over it like a vast and ghostly sentinel. Floating somewhere beyond sight of my house, I might reel in my supper, listen to the hiss of dolphins slicing past my strake, catch the sunlight's final strides up the mountains' peaks.

But the last time I spent any time in a motorboat I ended up, as I very nearly started out, hunched over the bow or the stern or whatever the hell it is, returning to the ocean the fish I had consumed the night before. I'm all right when a boat's speeding along, but when the engine's cut and the hull dips and weaves and bobs with each lapping swell in a fuming bloom of gasoline, the sweat prickles the back of my neck and my brow begins to freeze. I try to grip the horizon with both eyes and imagine my stomach bolted to a flat and immovable slab of concrete, and I start to taste, with each foreboding little belch, the bitter gall of Dramamine. If my captain, my host, hasn't yet read the warning signs and started up his engine and begun the lugubrious voyage back to shore, well, that's his problem: his boat, and my breakfast.

Hanging over the side of boats or locked in the rest rooms of airplanes or standing expectantly by the roadside, I've had a lot of time to think about nausea, and I've come to regard it not only as a last-ditch attempt to stop the world and disembark but as a kind of insight. After I've twirled my children around, or rolled down a hill, or turned my head suddenly on a speeding train, I think sometimes that the spinning sensation I get is no illusion. Dizziness is my inner ear's reluctant admission to what the rest of me already knows—that even if you bolted me and my Boston Whaler to Mount Rainier herself, we would be no less in motion: still pitching, rolling heedlessly in a vast black sea.

The Deck

THE old deck that came with the house had been a mini-
malist construction straight out of the pages of a 1960s handyman's manual, designed to get the most mileage out of the
least lumber on a weekend hardware binge. It seemed to
function all right, but looking up at it from the beach, you
could see how it had forsaken geometry for a kind of expres-
sionism, sagging in the rain like a laundry line. When I
crawled underneath to see what I could salvage, I found I
could stick my jackknife through almost every joist. The soft
rotted fir crumbled especially around the interstices where
twenty years of dirt and pine needles had wicked several
thousand gallons of Northwest rainfall into the unprotected
grain.

The deck ran halfway along the front of the house, facing
the channel, but it was a shadow of its former self. The original
deck, built with the house in 1905, ran its full sixty-foot
length and turned two corners. But even the original deck,
complete with rail and lattice plates, looks rickety and temporary in the early pictures of the house. The first story is
stone, and against its beach-rock facade even the most substantial wood structure looked like a rowboat foundered on
the Rock of Gibraltar.

So I decided to add three substantial stone piers to the

front of my new deck to "tie it in," as my neighbor put it, with the rest of the house. The handyman deck, diced and crowbarred, came down in a day, revealing a parched clay floor and mossy piles of lumber and trash. I dug and poured the footings for the piers myself, slopping together incremental loads of concrete in a wheelbarrow with shovel and hose and then leveling off each gray puddle with a plank. And after the mason came and mortared river rock into three matching, sculpted heaps, it took me three months of sawing and hauling and hammering to complete the deck itself.

I guess "complete" may not be the word for it. My construction projects, like my literary projects, are not completed so much as abandoned. (I know I'll get around to securing the knobs on the balustrades and nailing the trim along the lath to hide the aluminum hangers that now catch the evening light along the foremost joist. Just not this minute.) Nevertheless, if you don't look too closely, and if the weeds stand high enough in the yard, it not only appears complete but, if I do say so myself, looks as though it has been here forever.

We have installed a suite of already mildewed Chinese wicker furniture under the roofed porch that connects the deck to the front door, punctuated the row of balusters with Chinese pots from Vancouver, and set a pair of cedar Adirondack chairs out on the exposed deck, where they are weathering silver in the sun and the rain.

I am never so tall as when I walk on a floor of my own construction, and sometimes I stride the deck just to feel it underfoot, bouncing a little at the knees to test its disposition. It would seem I have earned the right to come to rest on one of the Adirondacks, to snooze awhile on the wicker settee, but the deck has begun to worry me, like a stage set for a play that can never be produced.

I wonder if I will ever fit into this house as nicely as my grandfather's piano or the Adirondack chairs. I keep telling myself that I don't yet fit because the house isn't complete, that once the lawn and garden take hold, and the resurrected climbing roses and wisteria begin to bloom again, and I have stripped the last piece of molding down to the close fir grain and sanded every floor and repainted every room and re-caulked every rippled windowpane, I will finally become the lord of this manor. But I think the problem is not that the house is incomplete but that I am incomplete, and I, and not the house, am in need of renovation.

I wonder if I'll ever grow in scale and confidence to suit my new home's rooms and vistas; if I will ever populate the front yard on Sunday afternoons with giggling children, and serve mint juleps and lemonade to a dozen of my friends and family on the shaded porch, and lead them on contemplative expeditions to and from the beach, as unhurried tall-masted sailing ships drift by at the whim of a gentle breeze.

The children who now come to visit gravitate toward the VCR that dominates what we wistfully call the library, and the last couple who came to sit on our deck asked for diet colas and bickered about childcare, and most of the traffic on the channel is composed of whining boats that zip by like hornets, skippered by broad men in caps and country club pastels and named after alcoholic second wives.

The deck, in fact the whole house, keeps giving me expectant looks, as if it still hungers for its lost acreage. Coming up to the beach in my boat some evenings, I can almost envision the house as it once was in the exalted solitude of its original five hundred acres, before the old place was subdivided and the surrounding yard shrank down to a single acre.

Reclaiming those acres would be a simple matter, it seems to whisper to me like Lady Macbeth. *What would it take? A little bribery, extortion, arson? Maybe a couple of homicides?* Nothing that would have daunted the Edwardian barons of its day.

But it's no accident that the estate shrank; it was too big to begin with. "The world can't afford the rich" says the bumper sticker, and the same might be said of their estates, maybe even of the ones they open to the public. On Bainbridge Island, for instance, there is something called the Bloedel Reserve, the retired estate of a lumber magnate comprising one hundred and fifty acres of gently tended gardens representing the horticultural arts of England, Europe, and Japan, all carefully integrating native trees, flowers, mosses, and grasses. If it is not exactly a shrine to nature, the Bloedel Reserve is at least an artful and benign memorial to the Bloedel family. But the paying visitors who stroll its dappled bark lanes are, of course, not encouraged to dwell on the fact that none of the exquisite plutographic glories of the Bloedel Reserve would have been possible without the decimation of one hundred and fifty but tens of thousands of acres of virgin forest.

So I shall ignore the hungry looks the house keeps giving me, and try to contain my nostalgia before it hemorrhages into nostomania: a lunatic craving for a past that, if it ever was, probably never should have been. But I shall always feel not settled so much as encamped in this house, a caretaker at its beck and call.

In Common

A *COUPLE* of months after we moved to Washington a friend of mine came visiting from New York and returned, shaking his head, from a day in Seattle. After buying a sweater from a soft-spoken and erudite personal shopper at Nordstrom's and downing a cup of Starbuck's espresso at a sidewalk coffee shop, he'd climbed aboard the bus to return to the ferry terminal, his shoulders hunched, his teeth clenched, his exact change locked in his fist, braced for a New York encounter with mass transit.

But the driver refused to take his money—for a stretch of downtown Seattle the bus ride is free—and he chirped a friendly good morning and then, discerning from my friend's consternation that he was an out-of-towner, asked if he needed any help getting to where he was going.

A little while later the driver spotted an elderly lady, obviously confused and, as it turned out, very nearly blind, standing a block from the nearest bus stop and waving her cane to get his attention. The driver stopped the bus, helped her climb aboard, showed her to a seat behind him, and every now and then, as he pointed out various municipal highlights to my friend, assured the old lady that he would announce her stop to her and see to it when she disembarked that she got headed in the right direction.

"That isn't a city," my friend groused when he got back to the island. "It's a goddamn theme park."

For a while it seemed to me that there was something to this, that somehow Seattle had escaped the division and alienation that plagues the rest of the country's cities. Just being a pedestrian was a kind of civics lesson for this émigré from the East. People never jaywalked, always stuck to the right, and even nodded and smiled to each other on streets, in stores and elevators. Drivers stopped to let pedestrians by, paused at yellow lights to avoid gridlock, and never honked their horns. (I didn't realize about honking horns until the first day I got behind the wheel in Seattle and sensibly honked mine at the sluggish old man in the car in front of me, and suddenly from every direction people were glowering at me.)

I attributed all this civility to Seattle's surroundings. It seemed to me that Seattle's setting is uniquely unifying because it is so remarkable that perfect strangers do in fact remark upon it to each other. I figured that people were bonded by their equal shares in the lakes and the sound and the mirror-image ranges of the Cascades and the Olympics, by the mysterious comings and goings of Mount Rainier: by the strangely soothing aspect of nature viewed from great distances.

But now I'm beginning to think that I was on the wrong track, and that what makes—or maybe by now it would be safer to say what *made*—Seattle so livable was that it simply hadn't yet reached its saturation point. It seems that in just these past three years Seattle's civility has declined, and lately the horns have begun to blare along its streets, the pedestrians have begun to collide and dart from the curbs and curse the taxicabs, the rush hour grids have begun to lock.

All this at a time when Seattle has been topping various national lists of Most Livable Cities. Of course, even if being named the most livable city in America were an honor these days, and it isn't, Seattleites still wouldn't welcome the attention. It's one of those designations that mark their own expiration, for it guarantees the kind of short-term and lopsided prosperity that afflicts other major cities: prosperity that brings with it condominiums and homelessness, great restaurants and hunger, private schools and dropouts, enclaves and crime waves, and every month a hefty charge for the best things in life that used to be free.

Courtesy of the media, Seattle's livability has become a kind of curse, and now people have been looking back to the aerospace industry crash of the 1970s with a certain wistfulness.

"Will the last person leaving Seattle please turn out the lights?" the sign by the Boeing plant used to say, and though nobody now hankers after unemployment, at least back then it seemed that Seattle might be overlooked—and therefore preserved—forever: shabby, bare-knuckled, provincial, but also authentic, neighborly, and safe from discovery, with enough time on its hands and gaps in its skyline to gaze at the lakes and the sound and the mountains.

Decline and Fall

IT'S been more than three years since I moved to the Great Northwest, and I've developed a bad case of what I call the Drawbridge Syndrome, an ailment that afflicts newcomers with a nagging inflammation of the proprietary gland. Rather than see ourselves as part of the problem of development and overpopulation out here, we aspire to be the last newcomers to Bainbridge Island, and as such become, like the oldest island residents, objects of local veneration, with perhaps a float of our own in the Fourth of July parade.

Sometimes when I think about the development that seems to be overtaking not only Bainbridge Island but the entire western region of Washington State, I have a hard time containing my despair. It extends not only to what is to come or to what is upon us but to the riches we've already squandered.

L. Rust Hills once envisioned America disassembling the infrastructure of its last hundred years or so and returning itself by the sweat of its brow to a simpler time he placed somewhere in the 1800s: not the good old days exactly but the old days informed by the best wisdom of the new.

In my darkest moments I have the feeling he may have been onto something, but I wonder if he took it far enough. If, as they keep telling us, the Northwest is really the last of the livable places in America—if, once this is gone, there will be nowhere else to dream about, nowhere else to run—then maybe we've reached the end of our history, or at least the end of our dream. Maybe it's time we took charge of our own decline—took charge of it the way we've always taken charge in this country—and made the decline and fall of the United States of America the best darn decline and fall the world has ever seen.

The way I see it, the beginning of this final interment of the American Dream would mark not the end of our history but its midpoint, for our nation's dismantlement would take at least as long as our first three hundred and fifty years of settlement, and it would have to be every bit as ingenious and audacious.

Think of it. Not only our cities and towns would have to come down, but our farms as well, and every canal and man-made lake would have to be drained, every rerouted river derouted, every regrade degraded, every road and track and runway peeled up like masking tape, every wire and cable rolled up like string. Factories constructed for the production of things would now devote themselves to the reduction of things all the way back to their source.

And so it would be on Bainbridge Island. And under the control and authority of the historical society, or perhaps the prehistorical society, I would break the windows of my house and grind them all back into sand, and I would pluck out the beach stones from my walls, one by one, and scatter them along the shore, tenderly coaxing the crabs back to their ancestors' shelters. The pipes and wires and nails and screws I would ship back to Pittsburgh to be turned to ore and tucked back into the Pennsylvania hills. And I would turn the studs and shingles to sawdust and chips and spew them around seedlings of madrona and fir.

And when I was done and all the rest of us were done, we would embrace each other and promise to write, and then we would sail back to Europe and Africa and Asia with the Statue of Liberty in tow, and wave to the grateful natives come to see us off from shore.

Beggars

THE first major business in Seattle was Yesler's Mill, which sat on the slope of Denny Hill, long since regraded to a modest angle but once a steep drop down to the bay. When lumber was brought west from the Cascades, the street that ran down to the mill was coated with fish oil and the logs skidded down like greased toboggans to be sawed into planks.

The street was otherwise so notable for its flophouses, brothels, and derelicts that its old name, Skid Road (or the bastardized Skid Row), became as synonymous with transient urban destitution as the Bowery in New York. Yesler's Mill is long gone and the neighborhood around it consists now of genteel shops and restaurants, but a good many derelicts still hang out in its interstices.

I mean to talk about the ambiguities of begging, as practiced by hoboes, winos, and bums: the bankrupted fishermen, the stranded sailors, the idle dockworkers, the useless cowboys and rootless Indians, the detrimental lumbermen, and the ruined, laid-off working men and women who beg in front of Seattle's department stores, share peach brandy on the benches, orate at the intersections, eat out of the trash barrels, piss in the flower beds, sleep in the Dumpsters.

I am not talking about the deinstitutionalized mentally ill, or the evicted families, or the single mothers and their hapless children and the teenage runaways who fend for themselves on the streets of Seattle. They do not present the same quandary, because their predicament is such an unqualified national shame.

I first confronted beggars as a boy growing up in New Delhi, India. I even came to know some of them by their nicknames, including Tata, a noseless leper who hung around our favorite fruit seller in Connaught Place.

As an American kid from Chicago, I initially had the impulse to give away whatever I had as I passed through the gantlets of beggars that lined my way. Drifting off to sleep, I would imagine myself bicycling through the beggars' encampments in Old Delhi, handing out stacks of rupee notes to the grateful, wretched multitudes.

But a lot of Indians claimed that the average New Delhi beggar took in more in a day than any bureaucrat could hope to earn in a month, that like pickpockets and prostitutes they were predatory, and formed a kind of caste all their own. Their rags were costumes, their grimaces contrived, their whining imprecations all sham and flimflam. *Don't give them anything,* I was always being told. *You'll only encourage them.*

Many Americans take a different route to the same conclusion. A lot of us believe that no one in this land of opportunity is a slave to circumstance. And so if people beg for a living, they must have chosen to beg for a living: chosen in some cases to abandon their families and squander their lives and drown their troubles in booze. By this reasoning that's their business, not ours; so don't give them anything, you'll only encourage them.

By means of Tata's upraised palm I became acquainted with the first moral quandary I'd ever encountered that wouldn't admit of certitude. So I picked my way through

the beseeching beggars, handing a few annas to some, plead-
ing bankruptcy to the rest, always angry and guilty and confused.

It was a relief to elude the horns of that dilemma when my
family moved back to the States. But my escape was only
temporary, for now beggars haunt the streets of every American city and are as unavoidable here as they once were in
New Delhi.

In New Haven they lingered on Broadway and Chapel
Street and on the central town green, and now in Seattle they
are everywhere: men and women posted every few hundred
feet, some with patient dogs and plaintive cardboard signs.
No job. No food. No home. Please give.

Out here they mask begging's abjection by calling it "pan-
handling," as though a beggar's life were colorful and rough-
and-tumble, like prospecting or oil rigging. I suppose the
term at least acknowledges the skill required to convince
those who are otherwise unmoved by a beggar's obvious
neediness that he at least has enough entertainment value to
deserve two bits.

But even if beggars find more dignity calling themselves
panhandlers, the purpose the sobriquet serves the rest of us
is to reinforce our suspicion that the beggar's circumstance
is wholly voluntary, and that the act of begging is a kind of
wily performance.

The fact is that begging often does involve a kind of scam,
and if the stakes were higher a lot of beggars could be thrown
into the clink for false advertising. But most beggars employ
their scams—the cups of coffee, the busfares out of town—
not because they don't really need the money but because
they've come to learn that there are only a few circumscribed
needs that move the majority of their fellow citizens. They
know that most of us would rather sober them up with a cup

of coffee than provide them with some hooch to keep the shakes at bay, that we'd rather buy them a ticket out of town than support our local flophouses.

In other words, they have come to know that most of us, when we are accosted, are moralizers who believe that the scabrous inebriate who asks us for a quarter is really asking for a solution to his problem, and that anything short of that—like, say, two bits toward a companionable swig of blackberry brandy—is a capitulation to the beggar's own wayward cravings.

And if in the process of begging a man lies to us as well, then there's an end to the transaction. But maybe it's unreasonable to assume that the destitute owe the prosperous their sincerity, or that we should expect of the down-and-out an abiding faith in the kindness of their fellowman. Two bits doesn't buy that much these days, and they wear enough of their pain on their sleeves as it is.

Like most people, I've tried to come up with a system by which to deal with the beggars who confront me on the city streets, a kind of defense policy by which I can determine the imprecations I might dignify with cash.

For a while I decided I wouldn't give any money to a lush. Then I figured I would ignore beggars who took up regular stations on the street. Then I excluded beggars who used dogs to gain the sympathy of passersby. Then, as Reagan began to do his worst, I decided I would reserve my spare change for the women and children who swelled the ranks of the homeless. And then I figured I would comfort myself with donations to shelters and storefront clinics and soup kitchens, and thus justify otherwise ignoring beggars altogether.

But for every rule I found too many exceptions, and I've begun to conclude that there can be no hard-and-fast rule about giving to beggars because there can be no hard-and-fast rules about any kind of human interaction.

It has proved a strenuous conclusion. From it I've evolved a kind of case-by-case approach that may in fact be feasible only for an idle, self-employed, and occasional visitor to the city. I have bought an old man a belt at a clothing store, for instance, and obtained a burger for another at McDonald's, and even when all I'm being thanked for is the petty beneficence of a little spare change, I've tried at least to look the poor beggar in the eye and acknowledge his mumbled thanks.

"You bet," I say, nodding back to him.

But it's my bet—a long shot—on him.

They Also Wait Who Stand and Serve Themselves

ANYONE interested in the future of American commerce should take a drive sometime to my old neighborhood gas station back in New Haven. Not that it is or ever was much of a place to visit. Even when I first moved to New Haven in 1974, it was shabby and forlorn: not at all like the garden spots they used to feature in the commercials, where trim, manicured men with cultivated voices tipped their visors at your window and asked what they could do for you.

Sal, the owner, was a stocky man who wore undersized, popped-button shirts, sagging trousers, and oil-spattered work shoes with broken laces. "Gas stinks" was his motto, and every gallon he pumped into his customers' cars seemed to take something out of him. "Pumping gas is for morons," he liked to say, leaning indelibly against my rear window and watching the digits fly on the pump register. "One of these days I'm gonna palm this place off on some Puerto Rican, move to Florida, and get into something nice, like hero sandwiches."

Sal had a nameless, walleyed assistant who wore a studded denim jacket and, with his rag and squeegee, left a milky film on my windshield as my tank was filling. There was a fume-crazed, patchy German shepherd, which Sal kept chained to the air pump, and if you followed Sal into his cluttered, overheated office next to the service bays, you ran a gantlet of hangers-on, many of them Sal's brothers and nephews, who spent their time debating the merits of the driving directions he gave bewildered travelers who turned into his station for help.

"I don't know," one of them would say, pulling a bag of potato chips off the snack rack, "I think I would've put 'em onto ninety-one, gotten 'em off at Willow, and then—bada-boom!—straight through to Hamden."

Sal guarded the rest room key jealously and handed it out with reluctance, as if something in your request had betrayed some dismal aberration. The rest room was accessible only through a little closet littered with tires, fan belts, and cases of oilcans. Inside, the bulb was busted and there were never any towels, so you had to dry your hands on toilet paper unless Sal was out of toilet paper, too.

The soda machine never worked for anyone except Sal, who, when complaints were lodged, would give it a contemptuous kick as he trudged by, dislodging warm cans of grape soda which, when their pop-tops were flipped, gave off a fine purple spray. Beside the snack rack in the office there was a machine that dispensed peanuts on behalf of the Sons of Garibaldi. The metal shelves along the cinder-block wall were sparsely stocked with cans of cooling system cleaner, windshield deicer, antifreeze, and boxed headlamps and oil filters. Over the battered yellow wiper case, below the Coca-Cola clock, and half hidden by a calendar from a janitorial supply concern, hung a little brass plaque from the oil company, awarded for Salvatore A. Castallano's ten-year business association.

I wish for the sake of nostalgia that I could say Sal was a craftsman, but I can't. I'm not even sure he was an honest man. I suspect that when business was slow he may have cheated me, but I never knew for sure because I don't know anything about cars. If I brought my old Volvo in because it was behaving strangely, I knew that as far as Sal was concerned it would never be a simple matter of tightening a bolt or reattaching a hose.

"Jesus," he'd wearily exclaim after a look under the hood. "Mr. Ward, we got problems."

I usually let it go at that and simply asked him when he thought he could have it repaired, because if I pressed him for details he would get all worked up.

"Look, if you don't want to take my word for it, you can go someplace else. I mean, it's a free country, you know? You got spalding on your caps, which means your dexadrometer's not charging, and pretty soon you're gonna have hairlines in your flushing drums. You get hairlines in your flushing drums and you might as well forget about it. You're driving junk."

I don't know what Sal's relationship was with the oil company. I suppose it was pretty distant. He was never what they call a "participating dealer." He never gave away steak knives or NFL tumblers or stuffed animals with his fill-ups, and never got around to taping company posters on his windows. The map rack was always empty, and the company emblem, which was supposed to rotate thirty feet above the station, had broken down long before I first laid eyes on it, and had frozen at an angle that made it hard to read from the highway.

If, outside of television, there was ever such a thing as an oil company service station inspector, he must have been appalled by the grudging service, the mad dog, the sepulchral john. When there was supposed to have been a gas shortage, Sal's was one of the first stations in the area to run out of gas, and a couple of years ago, during the holiday season, the company squeezed him out for good.

I don't know whether Sal is now happily sprinkling olive oil over salami subs somewhere along the Sun Belt. I only know that one bleak January afternoon I turned into his station to find him gone. At first, as I idled by the no-lead pump, I thought the station had been shut down completely. Plywood had been nailed over the service bays, Sal's name had been painted out above the office door, and all that was left of his dog was a length of chain dangling from the air pump's vacant mast.

But when I got out of the car I spotted someone sitting in the office with his boots up on the counter, and at last caught sight of the "Self-service Only" signs posted by the pumps. Now, I've always striven for a degree of self-sufficiency. I fix my own leaky faucets, and I never let the bellboy carry my bags. But I discovered as I squinted at the instructional sticker by the nozzle that there are limits to my desire for independence. Perhaps it was the bewilderment with which I approach anything having to do with the internal combustion engine; perhaps it was my conviction that fossil fuels are hazardous; perhaps it was the expectation of service, the sense of helplessness, that twenty years of oil company advertising had engendered—but I didn't want to pump my own gas.

A mongrel rain began to fall upon the oil-slicked tarmac as I followed the directions spelled out beside the nozzle. But somehow I got them wrong. When I pulled the trigger on the nozzle, no gas gushed into my fuel tank, no digits flew upon the gauge.

"Hey, buddy." A voice sounded out of a bell-shaped speaker overhead. "Flick the switch."

I turned toward the office and saw someone with Wild Bill Hickok hair leaning over a microphone.

"Right. Thanks," I answered, and turned to find the switch. There wasn't one. There was a bolt that looked a little like a switch, but it wouldn't flick.

"The switch," the voice crackled through the rain. "Flick the switch."

I waved as if I'd finally understood, but I still couldn't figure out what he was talking about. In desperation I stuck the nozzle back into my fuel tank and pulled the trigger. Nothing.

Through the window I could see that the man was now angrily pulling on a slicker. "What the hell's the matter with you?" he asked, storming by me. "All you gotta do is flick the switch."

"I couldn't find the switch," I told him.

"Well, what do you call this?" he wanted to know, pointing to a little lever near the pump register.

"A lever," I told him.

"Christ," he muttered, flicking the little lever. The digits on the register suddenly formed neat rows of zeros. "All right, it's set. Now you can serve yourself," he said, ducking back into the office.

As the gas gushed into my fuel tank and the fumes rose to my nostrils, I thought for a moment about my last visit to Sal's. It hadn't been any picnic: Sal claimed to have found something wrong with my punting brackets, the German shepherd snapped at my heels as I walked by, and nobody had any change for my ten.

But the transaction had dimension to it; I picked up some tips about color antennas, entered into the geographical debate in the office, and bought a can of windshield wiper solvent (to fill the gap in my change). Stations like Sal's had been a dime a dozen, but it occurred to me, as the nozzle balked and shuddered in my hand, that they were going the way of the village smithy and the corner grocer.

I somehow got a gob of grease on my glove as I hung the nozzle back on the pump, and it took me more than a minute to satisfy myself that I had replaced the gas cap properly. I tried to whip up a feeling of accomplishment as I headed for the office, but I could not forget Sal's dictum: Pumping gas is for morons.

The door to the office was locked, but a sign directed me to a stainless-steel teller's drawer which had been installed in the plate glass of the front window. I stood waiting for a while with my money in hand, but the long-haired man sat inside with his back to me, so at last I reached up and hesitantly knocked on the glass with my glove.

The man didn't hear me, or had decided, in retaliation for our semantic disagreement, to ignore me for a while. I reached up to knock again, but noticed that my glove had left a greasy smear on the window. Ever my mother's son, I reflexively reached into my pocket for a handkerchief and was about to wipe the grease away when it hit me: At last the oil industry had me where it wanted me—standing in the rain and washing its windshield.

Closing

*I*N the Spring of 1988, I went back to close on our old house in New Haven. We'd had the house appraised during a real estate boom, but by the time we put it up for sale the boom was on the wane, so the house was stalled on the market for ten months.

We'd had a nice life in the old place, but it was an odd house on the face of it. An abandoned and disintegrating school building of undetermined destiny stood behind it, and a three-story apartment building overlooked the postage-stamp backyard. The front door was on the side of the house, the entry squeezed by a narrow driveway, and the old roof was surfaced with expensive Florentine tiles that had cracked when I climbed out to patch the flashing around the chimney or tear down the rusted trunk of a TV aerial or caulk around the leaking window trim on the attic dormer. So for all its considerable charms, the house never exactly sold itself.

It was a little weird being back in my old hometown. I made the rounds of our friends and dropped in at my children's old day-care center and picked up a pizza from Sally's on Wooster Street. But I was strangely disoriented, as if visiting a parallel universe in which everything was identical to ours except that I had no family, and I had no home.

I closed on the house on a Friday, handing over keys and

documents, adjustment checks and handyman references and tips on beating the burglar alarm system to a couple in the throes of the usual last-minute qualms. It seemed to me, when my reassurances about the plaster and the sills and the newly asphalted roof failed to smooth their troubled brows, that closings, like births and deaths and marriages, might benefit more from the incantations of priests than the ministrations of attorneys.

Tucking my check into my jacket, I was driving past the house one last time, entertaining my own doubts and regrets, still missing my friends and family, still convinced of the obduracy of my Yankee stamp, when I decided to visit our next-door neighbors. They had recently divorced and the husband was not home, so I drove a couple of blocks to where his wife had moved. I rang the bell, but no one answered there, either, and as I was leaving a note in the door a woman called out to me with a frosty courtesy I had not encountered since we moved.

"Excuse me, young man," she said, "but is this by any chance your car?"

It's getting to be more and more flattering to be called "young man" these days, but the woman was no more than five or six years older than I: a sturdy, heavy-treading woman with straight-cut gray-brown hair that suggested the ears of the large mastiff she was leading and whose turd she was carrying home in a zip-lock bag.

"Uh, no," I told her. "It's a rental."

"Be that as it may," she said, "you've parked in front of my house."

"Ah," I said.

"And look," she said, stamping her foot on the sidewalk. "Look. Your—your *aerial* is stuck in the branches of my *tree*."

I walked over to the car, and we peered together at my aerial. It was in fact jutting in among some small branches of what looked to be a fairly recently planted cherry tree.

"Oh, *look* what you're doing to my tree," the woman said with a choking noise. "Retract it. Retract it at once."

I glanced down at the glowering mastiff and reached over and tried to retract the aerial for her, but it was one of those fixed jobs that didn't retract.

"I'm afraid it won't budge," I said.

"Then how do you propose to move your car without ruining my tree?"

"Uh, I guess I could back it out."

"No, you can't back it out. Look. Your aerial will chafe my branches."

"Chafe your branches?"

"Just look," she said, tenderly bending a twig toward her. "Look what you've done already."

I looked. I didn't see anything. "I don't see anything," I told her. "And," I ventured to say, "I don't quite see what you're getting so upset about."

"Oh, you don't?" she said, releasing the twig. "This is my tree, and you are damaging it. You had no *business* parking in front of my house in the first place."

"Listen, lady," I told her. "This is a public street."

"No, it's not," she said, rising to her full height. "This is a *neighborhood.*"

"Some neighborhood," I muttered, climbing into the car. "Now, would you like to hold the aerial down while I back out? Or shall we just take our chances?"

"You're not going to back out!" she said. "Don't you dare back out!"

I am usually forbearing in these situations, but this woman seemed to have arisen out of the ivied jungle of my old neighborhood, the precious, paranoid embodiment of every territorial dispute I'd ever had with my neighbors over garbage, children, dog shit, bicycles, broken branches, snow shoveling, hedge trimming, house painting, car parking, fence repairs: all undertaken with the special vehemence with which some of the most intelligent people in these United States suffer the slightest slings and arrows. A man's home is his castle on Prospect Hill, and everyone else is a serf.

And so at last I grinned with what I only hoped looked like a kind of homicidal glee as I backed past the angry woman, and my aerial swept through her twigs and sprang back into position with a lovely soft twang.

"I have your license!" she called out, shaking her zip-lock bag at me as I very slowly drove off down the street.

Riding back to the airport that evening, I couldn't tell if I was leaving home or heading home until we reached the Tappan Zee Bridge, and gazing through the passing cables at a row of clouds along the horizon, I caught myself wondering whether they were the Cascades or the Olympics, still covered over with snow.

The Movable Feast

As my family and I were approaching our first Christmas alone together in the Great Northwest, away from the rest of my relations, I began to hear the bells from the snowbound lanes of my boyhood and wondered how our Christmas here could ever measure up.

I never lived near my grandparents Ward, and so I don't imagine that my family celebrated Christmas at their house more than three or four times during my boyhood. But theirs was the definitive Christmas against which all others are still measured in my family. My grandparents' Christmas wasn't even particularly Christian so much as a celebration of family and abidance and continuity which, like Chanukah and all the irresistible festivals of light, induced in even their most irreligious descendants a hunger for ritual and remembrance.

All Christmas morning long my grandfather's house used to breathe the sleepy steam of roasting turkey. As we opened our presents, one at a time in the dappled glow of tree and hearth, Grandma's confections would already be circulating: almond crescents, addictive candied grapefruit rind, balls of chopped apricot rolled in sugar.

Now and then Grandma and Grandpa would be summoned from the tree by chattering timers to baste the turkey, reset the oven, put the sweet potatoes in to bake. And when all the presents were opened, Grandpa commenced what we called the "center ring cooking," decked out ostentatiously in an apron, sipping conspicuously from the mixing spoons, conducting with the baster.

"There's a lion in my kitchen," Grandma would declare as he worked at a portion of the counter he'd roped off for his artistry. Grandpa was a man of firm culinary convictions: about the consistency of gravy, the buoyancy of boiled onions, the clarity of roasting juices. But truth be known, he was merely the figurehead; my grandmother was the steady driving piston of the Christmas kitchen engine: paring, chopping, sautéing, stewing—a juggler of eggs and mixer blades and any grandchildren who insisted on making themselves useful.

A showboat exacts a certain toll from the rest of the fleet, and when the time came to carve the turkey, Grandpa was all theatrics and craft. He would make certain we were already seated with our eyes fixed on the kitchen door before he shouldered his way into the dining room carrying the grand brown bird on a heavy silver tray festooned with parsley.

He would lead us in a grace—a brief and ambiguous "Our Father, we thank Thee, amen"—and then he would ask whether we wanted breast or thigh.

"Of course in my day," he would declare, slashing his knife along an ivory-handled sharpener, "you couldn't say breast or thigh at the dinner table."

"Oh, *Clarence,*" Grandma would reply, looming like a giantess over the roofs and steeples of Grandpa's Christmas village.

I should explain. My grandfather Ward was an architectural historian and possessed, by his count, America's second-largest collection of F. AD. Richter & Co. stone building blocks, with which, at Christmastime, he used to construct winter scenes on the mantelpiece and cabinet tops of his large, chockablock house in Oberlin, Ohio.

His holiday masterpiece was the stone village he erected in the center of the dining table, including church and school and cemetery, dusted with false snow and minutely flanked by wire and bristle stands of pines. It was a village such as Dickens might have traveled in his dreams, and so perfect that as I peered at it at street level around the crystal stems of water glasses and along the tines of silver forks, I would not have been too surprised if Scrooge himself had appeared in a tiny doorway, stamping the powder from his boots.

Grandpa was always generous with strangers. "I am Clarence Ward and this is my family," he would have told Ebenezer, showing him to a perch on the saltcellar. "Someone pass Mr. Scrooge the relish tray."

"Now go ahead and start in," Grandpa always told us, poking at the air with a flesh fork as he doled out the slices of breast meat that seemed to fall from his knife like pages from a book. "Don't wait for me. It'll just get cold."

And so we would all start in, passing the cranberries over the china and silver and crystal, perhaps grazing the precarious stone steeples or puddling the town green with a slop of champagne. But by the time Grandpa had finally served himself, and all the fixings had been passed around again for his benefit, his eagle eye would alight on a grandson's already-empty plate.

"Geoff? It looks as though you could do with a little more turkey."

"Yes, thank you, Grandpa," my brother would say, passing back his plate. "It's all delicious."

"That's the boy," Grandpa replied, bending over the shredded bird. "Of course," he muttered, pouting slightly, "I haven't had my first bite yet."

We would debate the vices and virtues of Eisenhower and Oberlin faculty politics and the fruit harvest just past and the route we took to get there, while we consumed the white meat and dark meat and the yams and creamed onions and gravy and stuffing and cranberries and relishes, and then the plum pudding flaming blue and gold, with hard sauce so braced with brandy that it made my sister's eyes water. And when the dishes were done and the narcotic of turkey and champagne and hard sauce had kicked in, the adults dozed and we children dawdled, sated, in the far-flung reaches of the house.

The wiring was poor in my grandparents' house, and so the light was dim and rosy, and even if it was not so dim and rosy, it appears that way in the old slides Grandpa left behind as a proud record of his holiday productions. And so that is the glow my memory casts on all my holiday expectations, soft and hibernal and benign.

It fell to my mother to match those Christmases in the harsh efficient glare of real time, sometimes with my grandparents, her in-laws, attending. She made up her own secular traditions as she went along, and over the years they accumulated in my family into a daunting, inexorable holiday snowball. The day after she'd served, for the first time, a plum omelet for Christmas breakfast, she overheard my sister say to one of her friends, "Oh, yes. We *always* have plum omelets for Christmas breakfast." If in a burst of enthusiasm one year my mother set out home-baked cookies on the piano top, she would have to set out home-baked cookies on the piano top every year thereafter, and indeed, they had better be the same *kind* of home-baked cookies or at least one of her children or grandchildren might pout or mope or actually burst into tears.

Meddling daughters-in-law might persuade her to trim her

sails a little, in the interest of conserving her strength, or theirs, and a transient vegetarian might lobby, say, for zucchini lasagna in place of turkey. My father might even announce, perhaps as he was carving, that he never really liked turkey very much, that the whole holiday feast was too heavy and soporific, that we wasted a good deal of each other's company sleeping it off in the afternoon. But no rebels among us could stand for long in the snowball's path, or exorcise the ghosts of Grandpa's glistening Christmas village.

My father's carving was crippled by irony. He'd been his father's stagehand all his boyhood and had neither Grandpa's taste for the spotlight nor his knack with a carving knife. One year I saw a woman on television demonstrate how to carve a turkey. Remove the wings and legs first, she instructed, and then, starting on the leg end of the bird, carve the breast meat backward. So I passed this along to my father, who hates instructions, and he duly removed the legs and wings and set them aside. But when he turned back to carve, he couldn't for the life of him figure out where the wings had been and where the legs had been, and none of the rest of us could either. And so he guessed: badly, as it turned out, for the breast meat came off in shreds.

But it was on my parents' rooftop, not my grandparents', that I heard, indisputably, one Christmas Eve the runners of Santa's sleigh. And it was along my parents' table that I saw the family ebb and flow. First my brother's wife appeared at a chair beside my father, and then my nephew Nathan and my niece Kelly moved from high chairs to center chairs along the table sides. And then my wife, Debbie, sat herself to my father's left, and then Grandpa asked to be excused, giving his chair to my son, Jake. And then Grandma left us too, and along came my daughter, Casey. After seventeen helpings my brother's wife excused herself from the family table, and his second wife, Diane, took her place, and their boy, Garrett, joined us, and my sister's husband, Allen, and this year their son, Daniel, grinned at us all from a high chair through a fistful of yams.

My clan is composed of some of the most ferociously autonomous people I know, but something there is about the family feast that emulsifies us. Maybe it's because it requires that each of us be so many different things at once. In my case I must be son and little brother and big brother and brother-in-law and uncle and husband and father, in alternation or combination, depending on the seating arrangement. I may play uncle superbly with my niece, but my wife will think I'm reverting while my father will think I'm putting on airs.

Trying to be myself with the whole clan gathered is a more or less hopeless proposition. In this respect the roles of patriarch and matriarch are probably the least complicated, because everyone else is expecting more or less the same thing from them. It's the rest of us who must flirt with schizophrenia, floundering for perches on the flimsy outer branches of the family tree.

We have battled, sometimes bitterly, over how many gifts are too many, how many gifts are too few. Whenever a couple of us plead poverty or the press of business, we adopt new gift-giving systems—drawing names by lot, giving only to the next generation down, giving only within each family branch, and so forth—and manage merely to alternate between wretched excess and remorse. Even if we have seen each other once or twice a week over the past year, we are expected to behave as though this were an annual reunion. We bring to the holiday a collision of agendas, and occasionally someone will retreat in tears or wander muttering into the yard: perhaps no one touched the fruitcake, or the tree lights went on the blink, or we jubilated too halfheartedly singing carols by the tree. With fourteen of us jammed together the holiday feast and all its surrounding rituals seemed almost a setup sometimes, a guarantee that someone somehow was bound to be disappointed.

For our first Christmas alone together in the Great Northwest Debbie and the kids and I bought a little Douglas fir from an elderly Japanese lady at one of the island's dwindling tree farms. After the usual debates over height and angle we set it in the living room and festooned it with strings of lights and twenty years' worth of decorations: my son's and daughter's foil and paper day-care projects, crumbling papier-mâché animals from India, strings of wood shavings and popcorn and beads, and memorial cookie dough portraits of good old Ralph and his sister Dolores.

Out of a belief, I think, that the familiar would only remind us of the strangeness of our new surroundings, we displaced the traditional turkey with a slab of king salmon barbecued on the deck in the mild northwestern winter damp. And to this interloper at the family feast Debbie added her mother's persimmon pudding and corn bread, and our neighbors joined us, bearing pies for dessert.

I used to feel bad for people who couldn't or wouldn't congregate en masse with their extended families at Christmas and Chanukah. Out of an apprehension that I would have no self if I did not play all seven roles at Yuletide, celebrating family without the family seemed a bleak proposition, with no cookies on the piano, no plum omelet for breakfast, and now and again, in the pauses among presents, as coffee was fetched and wrappings collected, I did think of my other family gathered back in my parents' house so many miles and landscapes and states of mind away.

But our Northwest Christmas turned out fine. It was sweetly peaceable playing only two out of the seven roles

Christmas once demanded of me—husband to my wife, father to my children—and the Yuletide spotlight beamed where it was intended, upon my son and daughter.

My own children probably won't remember this first northwestern Christmas in their dreams. Their dreams of Christmas will always be of their grandparents' Christmas: jostling among their cousins in the path of my mother's Yuletide snowball, glimpsing their own destinies in the postures and poses and crotchets of their kin. But now I wonder if in my turn I might yet become holiday impresario to my own grandchildren, and exist beyond my lifetime in the same rosy retrospective glow.

But now I hear Debbie's timer ringing, and I must join the family at the table. So blessings on you, and the constancy of family and the abidance of friends, and whichever of the winter lights you praise.

Acknowledgments

I want to thank Kathryn Court, my editor at Viking, for all her help and encouragement; Peter Breslow of National Public Radio for broadcasting many of these pieces on *All Things Considered;* and Richard Todd, formerly of the *Atlantic Monthly,* not only for urging me to try my hand at essays early on in my career but for actually publishing the results.

We would debate the vices and virtues of Eisenhower and Oberlin faculty politics and the fruit harvest just past and the route we took to get there, while we consumed the white meat and dark meat and the yams and creamed onions and gravy and stuffing and cranberries and relishes, and then the plum pudding flaming blue and gold, with hard sauce so braced with brandy that it made my sister's eyes water. And when the dishes were done and the narcotic of turkey and champagne and hard sauce had kicked in, the adults dozed and we children dawdled, sated, in the far-flung reaches of the house.

The wiring was poor in my grandparents' house, and so the light was dim and rosy, and even if it was not so dim and rosy, it appears that way in the old slides Grandpa left behind as a proud record of his holiday productions. And so that is the glow my memory casts on all my holiday expectations, soft and hibernal and benign.

It fell to my mother to match those Christmases in the harsh efficient glare of real time, sometimes with my grandparents, her in-laws, attending. She made up her own secular traditions as she went along, and over the years they accumulated in my family into a daunting, inexorable holiday snowball. The day after she'd served, for the first time, a plum omelet for Christmas breakfast, she overheard my sister say to one of her friends, "Oh, yes. We *always* have plum omelets for Christmas breakfast." If in a burst of enthusiasm one year my mother set out home-baked cookies on the piano top, she would have to set out home-baked cookies on the piano top every year thereafter, and indeed, they had better be the same *kind* of home-baked cookies or at least one of her children or grandchildren might pout or mope or actually burst into tears.

Meddling daughters-in-law might persuade her to trim her

winter scenes on the mantelpiece and cabinet tops of his large, chockablock house in Oberlin, Ohio.

His holiday masterpiece was the stone village he erected in the center of the dining table, including church and school and cemetery, dusted with false snow and minutely flanked by wire and bristle stands of pines. It was a village such as Dickens might have traveled in his dreams, and so perfect that as I peered at it at street level around the crystal stems of water glasses and along the tines of silver forks, I would not have been too surprised if Scrooge himself had appeared in a tiny doorway, stamping the powder from his boots.

Grandpa was always generous with strangers. "I am Clarence Ward and this is my family," he would have told Ebenezer, showing him to a perch on the saltcellar. "Someone pass Mr. Scrooge the relish tray."

"Now go ahead and start in," Grandpa always told us, poking at the air with a flesh fork as he doled out the slices of breast meat that seemed to fall from his knife like pages from a book. "Don't wait for me. It'll just get cold."

And so we would all start in, passing the cranberries over the china and silver and crystal, perhaps grazing the precarious stone steeples or puddling the town green with a slop of champagne. But by the time Grandpa had finally served himself, and all the fixings had been passed around again for his benefit, his eagle eye would alight on a grandson's already-empty plate.

"Geoff? It looks as though you could do with a little more turkey."

"Yes, thank you, Grandpa," my brother would say, passing back his plate. "It's all delicious."

"That's the boy," Grandpa replied, bending over the shredded bird. "Of course," he muttered, pouting slightly, "I haven't had my first bite yet."